Answer Came There None

Books by E. X. Ferrars

Answer Came There None

E. X. FERRARS

A Perfect Crime Book
DOUBLEDAY
New York   London   Toronto   Sydney   Auckland

A Perfect Crime Book

PUBLISHED BY DOUBLEDAY

a division of Bantam Doubleday Dell Publishing Group, Inc.
666 Fifth Avenue, New York, New York 10103

DOUBLEDAY is a trademark of Doubleday,
a division of Bantam Doubleday Dell Publishing Group, Inc.

Library of Congress Cataloging-in-Publication Data

Ferrars, E. X.
Answer came there none / E. X. Ferrars. — 1st ed.
p. cm.
"A perfect crime book."
I. Title.
PR6003.R458A83   1993
823'.912—dc20   92-35631
CIP

ISBN 0-385-46856-3
Copyright © 1992 by M. D. Brown
All Rights Reserved
Printed in the United States of America
April 1993
First Edition in the United States of America

1   3   5   7   9   10   8   6   4   2

CHAPTER 1

'Please sit down, Mrs Marriott,' General Schofield said. 'May I give you a glass of sherry?'

'Thank you.'

Sara Marriott sat down on one of the dark red leather-covered chairs beside the empty fireplace. She felt intensely shy of the dignified old man who was busying himself with the decanter and glasses in a corner of the room, but shyness was an affliction that had troubled her all her life and worse than ever during the last few months, since the final break-up of her marriage. It was as if a threat always hovered in the air, particularly when she met a stranger, that she might be compelled to explain, actually to go into details, concerning her solitary condition.

The fact that it never happened did not exorcise the fear. Even though she was aware that most of her trouble came from the fact that really she wanted to talk about her personal disaster, that there was nothing else that she truly wanted to talk about, that knowledge did not help much. She sat stiff and silent, waiting for the glass of sherry to be put into her hand.

She was twenty-six, a tall, slim young woman with a pale, oval face which might have had a certain beauty if she had ever allowed it to give any clue to her emotions, hazel eyes and light brown, curly hair, which she wore cut short, showing a delicately modelled head. For her interview with General Schofield she had dressed in a neat grey linen suit with nothing about her that anyone was likely to remember except perhaps her small gold earrings. If she had known that the very simplicity of her appearance made her to some extent conspicuous it would have filled her with alarm.

'I hope you like dry sherry,' the General said. 'I'm afraid it's all I have.'

'Thank you,' she said again. 'It's what I always have myself.'

He brought her the glass and sat down with his own in the leather chair facing hers across the fireplace. The room was a square one with a high ceiling, two tall sash windows that overlooked the High Street, which was busier than usual that morning because it was market day, a roll-top desk, some bookshelves, dark brown velvet curtains and a dark brown carpet, dotted here and there with bright Persian rugs. The pictures on the walls were mostly photographs of young men in uniform.

'Of course you think I'm an old fool,' the General said. 'At my age I ought to know better.'

His age, she had been told, was eighty-three. He was tall, over six foot, and did not stoop much. He was wide-shouldered and spare. His white hair was still thick and his bushy eyebrows were almost black. The eyes beneath them were a pale, bright blue. His face was long and narrow with the kind of tan acquired by years spent in foreign places, under hot suns, the kind of tan that never fades beyond a certain sallowness. He was wearing a dark blue blazer and twill trousers. His tie had stripes which Sara thought meant that it was probably regimental, or perhaps belonged to an even earlier time of his life and the public school where it had certainly started.

'As a matter of fact,' she said, 'it's mostly people who are in their eighties, or even their nineties, who feel they're qualified to do what you want to do. Or perhaps it's only they who feel they might benefit by some help from me. Younger people may feel they can manage by themselves.'

'So you've done a good deal of this kind of thing before, have you?'

Either the sherry or the kindness in the old man's voice was beginning to make Sara relax a little. She no longer sat quite so stiffly in her chair or felt so frightened.

'Not so very much, actually,' she said. 'Just now and then, when something interesting comes up. But now I've got to earn a living and I'm glad of any chance to do it. My marriage broke up recently, you see, so I need to work. I haven't really any choice.'

So there it was as usual, it was she who had introduced the forbidden subject. It was not really necessary for her to explain why she had to earn a living, yet it always seemed to be something that had to be brought out into the open.

'Dear, dear, I'm sorry,' General Schofield said, as people always said, when she only wished that someone would say that he was glad to hear that the matter at least was settled and that she must be feeling very relieved that it was all over. 'But you've a right to some maintenance, haven't you? Not that I know much about those things.'

'I'd sooner be independent.'

'And work like this, you really find it interesting?'

'Sometimes, very. Sometimes very irritating. Sometimes nothing in particular.'

'Well, I hope you won't feel you're wasting your time with me, because truly I've had a very interesting life. But I can understand it if you feel that I ought to be able to make an interesting book out of it myself, without having to employ a ghost.'

'Shall we call it a collaborator?'

He gave a little bark of laughter, as if that pleased him.

'Yes, of course. And naturally your name will be on the title-page with mine and that isn't how it is with a ghost, is it? But if your name weren't there, who that knows me would believe that I'd written the thing myself? All my old friends would laugh themselves sick at the idea. But how did you start on this work?'

'My husband's in publishing,' she said, 'and I used to do a little writing on my own, short stories and the occasional bit on travel and so on, and it occurred to him one day to push a job of this sort my way and see how I managed. And I did rather well with it and the publisher was pleased. It was the life-story of someone who had started life as a minor film star and ended up as a drug-taking prostitute. And even when my husband left the firm and joined another, those first people kept pushing work my way. That's how it was arranged that I should work for you. But if you aren't satisfied, of course you must tell me.'

'I'm sure I shall be satisfied. I'm sure we shall get on very well together. I only hope you won't find it a terrible bore. Can the life-story of an old army man who's never taken drugs or pushed them, or even had anything to do with spies or anything like that, be nearly as fascinating as the life-story of a prostitute? But stories of the old Empire days are rather coming into fashion, aren't they? I was born in Burma, you know, and I've spent most of my life abroad. I only retired here to Edgewater after my dear wife died, because it's the place where I spent a good deal of my childhood when my parents—my father was in the army too—thought I ought to be receiving an English education. I lived here in this house with an aunt who eventually left it to me, and I always had a certain sentiment for the place. I was sent here too young to have any memories of the Rangoon of those days, though I returned there later. But that reminds me, where are you staying? Have you found a room for yourself?'

'I've taken a room in the Red Lion for a night or two,' she answered, 'but I can't stay there, it's too expensive. I must look for lodgings somewhere.'

'Ah, the Red Lion,' he said and his pale blue eyes lit up

with amusement. 'D'you know what one of my first memories of this country is? It's actually of that Red Lion where you're staying. My mother and I stayed in it for a few nights while my aunt was getting my room ready for me. I was only four years old at the time. And it worried me very much that the place should be called the Red Lion when the whole building was painted pale green. It's had a good many colour changes since those times. For a while it was a dreary sort of chocolate colour, and now of course it's white with rather a lot of very black beams that don't look too genuine, but I think pale green was the best. It's very old, you know. Pepys mentions it. He stayed there once and praised the food.'

'It's still very good, but it is expensive.'

'So sophisticated too, compared with what it used to be. A fashionable hotel, when it used to be just a country pub. But you'd like something comfortable. Tell me, how would a small furnished flat suit you? It's only just occurred to me that I know of one that's available. And I don't think the rent would be very high. But of course you'd have to look after yourself, cook your own meals and so on. There wouldn't be any service. How does that strike you?'

'If it's really something that I can afford, it sounds excellent.'

'I know it's just become vacant,' he said. 'It's on the top floor of the house of an old friend of mine, Mrs Cannon. As a matter of fact, it's just across the road from the Red Lion, a big square house which you may have noticed. Althea Cannon is the widow of the man who for years was by far the best doctor in Edgewater. They moved into the house when they were quite young and he had his consulting rooms on the ground floor and they lived on the floor above. And of course in those days they had servants living on the top floor. And when he died she didn't want to move, so she had the house converted into three flats. She and her son live on the ground floor and the one above it, and some young man whose name I forget has the basement, and until recently a young couple had the top floor, but I know they've just left to go to some job in New Zealand, so she wants another tenant. I don't think she's fixed up anything yet. I've been up there once or twice. The place is quite small, just two rooms with a little kitchen and a bathroom, and it's very simple, but I believe it's got everything you'd need. And it's only a few minutes' walk away from here, which you might find an advantage. Or have you perhaps a car?'

'Yes, I've a car, but it would be nice to be near,' Sara said. 'But won't it be rather expensive?'

'I don't think so, if Mrs Cannon takes to you. Having the kind of tenant she likes means more to her than the rent she can get. But if the idea doesn't appeal to you, you could look in the *Edgewater Advertiser*. You may find plenty of addresses there.'

'I'd like to call on Mrs Cannon straight away, if you think I might do that, and see if the flat's available.'

'Good, good. I'm sure she'll let you have it. You won't be giving rowdy parties, will you, or turning the television on so loud that it maddens her, or setting the place on fire by throwing burning cigarette ends in the wastepaper basket?'

'I don't smoke.'

He laughed. 'I'm sure you'll be just what she wants. But she's had experience of all those things I mentioned and it's made her cautious. She and her son Oliver are very quiet. He's a lecturer at the Edgewater Agricultural College, and he's a very clever man, I believe, though I don't understand anything about his work. You'll soon find I'm not at all a clever sort of man myself. That's why I need your help, of course. But I'm sure that's going to turn out a pleasure. Now when shall we begin?'

'Tomorrow?' Sara suggested.

He looked delighted. 'You can really manage that? If you'd like longer to get settled, just say so.'

'Time's valuable,' she answered. 'If you're ready to start, let's get ahead with it.'

'Very well then, suppose you arrive here about nine o'clock. No, let's say ten. I'm never at my best too early. You'll take a lot of notes, I suppose.'

'If you don't mind, I'll use my tape-recorder. It's better than my shorthand.'

'A tape-recorder? I hadn't thought of that.' He looked a little uneasy. 'I've never really managed to keep pace with all these modern gadgets. I wonder if I shall feel self-conscious, knowing that everything I say is being recorded. I'd thought of our just chatting, and you taking a note or two when it was needed.'

'That's really how it will be,' Sara reassured him. 'You'll soon forget the thing.'

'I suppose so. But now tell me a little about yourself. You're soon going to know a great deal about me, a lot of it very boring, I expect, though those are the bits you'll cut out. But I'd like to know a little about you. Have you any family?'

She had felt that that question, in some form or other, would come sooner or later, if perhaps not so directly, but some degree of curiosity about her was sure to show itself. Her clients, if that was the right word for them, were after all about to reveal a great deal about themselves to her, and the question of her capacity to understand them and to handle their confidences in a way that they thought was fitting was not unimportant to them.

She had some stock answers ready for this when the occasion arose, but today she felt less sure than usual that they would be altogether adequate. Something about the old man in the chair facing her in his sombre brown room

and with the glass of sherry in his hand and with his singularly appealing smile seemed to demand of her something
more personal than usual. But she had never had the habit
of responding easily to strangers, so she said what she
generally said.

'Have I any children, do you mean?'

'Well, have you?'

'No.'

'But parents? You're a young woman. Are your parents
living?'

'My father died when I was ten,' she answered, 'and my
mother married again. She married an American and they
live in Connecticut. He's a professor at Yale.'

'Ah, so you know America quite well.'

'I've been over a few times.' The truth was that she had
been over a fair number of times, but not at all since the
break-up of her marriage, though her mother had taken to
writing more often than usual, urging her to come. She
would have been very kind too, if a little patronizing towards a young woman who had not been able to keep her
husband, and Sara was fond of her stepfather and could
have talked to him more easily than to her mother about
what had happened. But before exposing herself to their
kindness she felt that it was imperative that she should have
learnt to stand on her own feet. She knew that they might
be hurt by her rejection of their efforts to help her, but
could not convince herself that this mattered.

'It's many years since I was there last,' General Schofield
said. 'Most of my travelling was in the Far East and in
Africa. People tell me that New York has changed very
much in recent years, as London has. The London I knew
as a young man has almost vanished. You live in London,
I believe.'

'No, I've a little flat in Windsor. Convenient for London,
where I do a good deal of my work. And I spent most

of my childhood there and used to feel that I'd never want to live anywhere else. But I don't think I'd care for it now.'

'Where did you go to school?'

'Oddly enough, in a place quite near here. It's called Granborough. It's a coeducational school and I believe was once thought very progressive, though I expect lots of other schools have quite overtaken it by now.'

'Now that's very interesting,' the General said. 'That young man I mentioned, the one who lives in Mrs Cannon's basement, the one whose name I can't remember, he teaches at that school. Perhaps you'll find that a bond. So Edgewater isn't actually strange to you. You'll have come into the town occasionally, I expect.'

'Just now and then. If a friend had parents down on a visit, probably staying at the Red Lion, one might be invited out for tea.'

'You won't find it's changed as much as most places nowadays. I suppose it's a little off the beaten track, though of course it's got chain stores and suburbs and council estates that weren't here when I was a boy. I hope the idea of coming back to it attracted you.'

Actually it had been one of the things that had almost made her refuse to tackle the job of the old man's memoirs. She was not in the market for memories just at present. The more she could forget, she thought, and the more new things she could discover, the better for her. However, she had needed the money.

'Then did you go to a university?' he asked.

'Yes, London,' she answered. 'I did English Literature at University College.' And had met the man she married, though there was no need to add that.

'So you're a very well-educated young lady and you're going to find me an ignorant old bore. I know perfectly well, you know, that people like me shouldn't suddenly think of writing their memoirs. It's a kind of egotism. Yet as I said, I do feel I've had an interesting life and that it could be worth while to write about it before the world I knew is wholly forgotten, or left to scholars to dig up in another hundred years' time. Things I remember as if they happened only yesterday are already just ancient history to someone of your age. Yet they may come to seem important to people who are younger still.'

Sara felt inclined to say that she believed that everyone had had an interesting life, that the mere act of living could not avoid being interesting, but that it was only a few who were capable of making that evident in words. She finished her sherry and stood up, and he stood up too and they shook hands and he showed her out through the small, dark hall into the street.

It was dazzling with the brilliant sunshine of a cloudless August morning. The front door opened straight on to the pavement, only a single step above it. The house, she thought, looked as if it might have been built in the seventeenth century. Most of the centre of the town was old, though here and there, as General Schofield had said, the chain stores had moved in and there was a square red bank that might have been built in Edwardian days just opposite his house. The High Street was not really very wide, yet it looked wider than it was because there were no tall buildings along it. At one end it led into the market square, which today was full of stalls of brightly coloured things, fruit and vegetables and knitted goods and rolls of cloth and children's toys. A good deal of shouting by people crying their wares reached her as she stood deciding which way to turn. At the far end the street led to the Red Lion and a street which led to a junction with the motorway to London. That was new since she had been here last. There had been no motorway then, only a meandering road that did in the end lead to London and so naturally was called the London Road.

It was across this street, facing the old inn, that the square brick house stood that belonged to General Schofield's friend, Mrs Cannon, and it was to this, Sara decided, that it would be sensible to go now, unless she were to look first for somewhere to have lunch. She hesitated, then started towards Mrs Cannon's house.

Its door, like that of General Schofield, opened straight on to the pavement, though beside it there was a railing and a gate and steps going down to the door of the basement. The house was built of the rosy brick that the Georgians had favoured, and its door was white with an elegant fanlight above it. There were two bells let into the door frame, the lower one with a card beside it with the name Cannon on it, and the upper one with a space from which a card, presumably, had recently been removed. Sara pressed the lower bell.

The door was not actually closed and was flung open so instantly that it could not have been in answer to her ring. Someone had just been about to pull it open and come out, and had indeed started to do so before realizing that Sara was standing in the way. It was a man who looked as if he were in a great hurry. He gave a little gasp of surprise at seeing her, frowned as if it were irritating to have to stand back, and said querulously, 'Yes?'

He was a tall man with thick, dark hair, a square, heavy-featured face, wide-spaced dark eyes and a mouth that was wide but with tight-looking, narrow lips. He was wearing flannel trousers, a grey cardigan and an open-necked shirt. He looked about forty.

But what Sara noticed about him particularly was that his cheeks were very flushed and that there was a blaze of excitement or anger in his eyes.

'I believe there's a flat to let here,' Sara said. 'Can I speak to Mrs Cannon?'

He turned and shouted at a closed door behind him, 'Mother, someone about the flat!'

Then he thrust his way past Sara and strode off along the High Street.

The door facing her was evidently something that had been installed when the house had been converted into flats. A fine staircase went up beside it, but what must once have been a spacious hall had been split in half by a partition of white-painted panelling. Sara was just about to ring again when she realized that the door in the panelling was ajar and that someone was looking at her through the opening.

She waited a moment, then stepped forward and said, 'Mrs Cannon?'

The door was opened further and a small old woman stood looking at her thoughtfully, then said, 'You're Mrs Marriott.'

She looked about eighty, had thin white hair fluffed up above her forehead to make as much of it as possible, a round, plump, deeply wrinkled face, dark eyes and a little pouting mouth, touched up with lipstick. Except that she had slender, shapely legs and very small, bony hands, she was plump all over, though she was carefully corseted to control this. She was wearing a well-cut grey skirt of heavy silk, a high-necked black blouse and a necklace made of several strands of gold links. If she had not exactly an air of elegance, she at least gave an impression that no expense had been spared.

'Come in,' she said.

Sara was surprised that the old woman had known who she was, then realized what must have happened.

'General Schofield telephoned you to say I'd be coming, did he?' she said.

'A few minutes ago,' Mrs Cannon said, closing the door

behind Sara as she entered the flat. 'You're going to be working with him, I believe.'

The strange thing about the little woman, who had the air of someone who would normally be very self-possessed, was that her voice was shaking. Also, as they entered a large drawing-room where the light was brighter than in what was now the partitioned-off hall, Sara saw that the flush on Mrs Cannon's cheeks was natural and not a result of make-up. She seemed oddly flustered and excited, which made Sara think of what had been almost the same in the man who had hurried past her a moment before. He was obviously her son, for apart from calling out to someone whom he had addressed as his mother, there was a good deal of resemblance between them.

'General Schofield is an old friend of mine,' Mrs Cannon said. 'We've known each other for many years. I think it's ridiculous of him to think of writing his memoirs now, especially as he can't manage it by himself, but I suppose it will help him to pass the time. Old age is very boring. I hope you'll be capable of sorting out his ideas for him.'

She was peering at Sara curiously. The shake had gone from her voice, but it was shrill and harsh, and the high colour had not left her cheeks.

'Sit down,' she said, 'and let us discuss the flat. How long do you think you might want it for? I shouldn't like to let it for less than three months.'

'I don't really know how long I'll be staying in Edge-water,' Sara said as she sat down in an easy chair near the window. 'That depends on how things work out with General Schofield.'

Most of the furniture in the room was Victorian except for some comfortable, cretonne-covered chairs and a sofa, and there was a good deal too much to seem appropriate in the high, airy room that belonged to at least a century earlier. Its windows overlooked a small walled garden, very

formally laid out with paved paths, lavender hedges and
rose-beds and with a sundial in the centre. From her bedroom in the Red Lion across the street, Sara had already
had a glimpse of the garden over its high wall.

Mrs Cannon had begun to walk about the room. She
seemed possessed by a nervous restlessness. But suddenly
she paused, looking not at Sara but into a mirror over the
fireplace and, speaking to her own reflection as if it were to
someone with whom she had been arguing, said, 'Ah yes,
that's it—that's what I'll do. That'll settle things.'

She gave a rather eerie little chuckle, then resumed her
walking, then stopped again, but this time facing Sara.

'Please forgive me,' she said. 'I'm not behaving very well,
but I've had a shock and I'm not quite myself.' She drew
a chair near to Sara's and sat down. 'But I know what I
must do. I've quite made up my mind. Quite. I've known
for some time I might have to do something of the sort,
sooner or later, but I've always put the thought away from
me. But now I know. That woman shan't get her hands on
anything. Now about this flat . . .' For a moment she looked
bewildered, as if she did not know why they should be
talking about a flat, but then she drew a deep breath and
let it out in a long, sad sigh. 'You'd like to see it, I suppose,
before we talk about the rent and so on.'

'If I've come at an inconvenient time,' Sara said, 'I could
go away and perhaps come back later. Or if General Schofield was wrong that you want to let it, I'm sorry to have
bothered you.'

'Oh, I want to let it, yes,' Mrs Cannon said, 'and of
course his recommendation means a great deal to me. We're
old friends—oh, I've told you that already, haven't I? I
know I repeat myself a lot nowadays. And I'll get Mrs
Worth to take you up there in a minute. I'm not too fond
of going up all those stairs myself. Mrs Worth's my daily
help. She comes in five days a week and stays till she's got

my lunch for me. She'd probably do your cleaning for you
if you wanted her to. She used to do it for my last tenants.
And of course she'd clear up the place for you before you
moved in. They only left yesterday and I haven't been up
there since they went, so I don't know what state it's in,
but they were nice, careful people. When would you like to
move in?'

'Perhaps if I could see it first . . .'

'Yes, of course, of course, I'm not thinking. It's this shock
I've had. Not that anyone is going to understand why it's
such a shock and they'll all be against me. They'll tell me
I'm quite in the wrong. But when you've given your whole
heart to something for years and you thought everyone was
happy . . . But you won't want to hear about that. You
want to see the flat. Just wait a minute and I'll get Mrs
Worth.'

She was soon back, accompanied by a tall, thin woman
in black trousers and a bright pink shirt. She looked about
fifty, muscular and quick-moving, with thick grey hair, grey
eyes and a good-natured smile.

'You want to see the flat,' she said. 'Come along, then.
The lunch is in the oven, so I mustn't be long, but I can
take you up.'

'Thank you.'

Sara stood up and followed the tall woman out into the
hall. They went out from it and into what was left of the
entrance hall of the house, then up the staircase with its
fine wrought-iron banisters, which must once have been the
main stairway of the house, then reached a landing and
then went higher still. Sara remembered that General Schofield had told her that Mrs Cannon and her son lived on
the two lower floors of the house, and as their apartment
appeared to be self-contained, she wondered for a moment
how they managed to climb from one floor to the other,
then she realized that in a house of this class there had

almost certainly been a second staircase for the servants and that it must be this that the Cannons had retained for themselves.

Reaching a landing on the top floor, Mrs Worth pushed open a door and went through it, holding it open for Sara. It had not been locked. It led straight into a room of medium size with two small dormer windows and a sloping ceiling. Two other doors opened out of the room. As they were both standing open Sara could see that one led into a small kitchen and the other into a bedroom. The furniture was modern and cheap, but simple and quite pleasant. Two easy chairs were covered in black imitation leather. There was a television and a telephone with an answer-phone and there were some flower prints on the white walls. It all looked sufficiently comfortable and convenient and easy to look after.

'The bathroom's through here,' Mrs Worth said, and when she had given Sara a minute to look around and had led the way into the bedroom, in which there was a double bed with a candlewick bedspread and a built-in wardrobe and dressing-table, she opened a door into a small pale blue bathroom. 'It's ever so nice, I always think. I wish our own house was anything like it, but my husband—he drives a lorry—wouldn't ever be without his garden. It was Mr Oliver who arranged it all when Dr Cannon died and Mrs Cannon decided to stay on and convert the house into flats. And she's a wonderful lady, ever so kind. You mustn't let what you heard just now put you off. It only happens now and then and it's best not to take any notice.'

'What I heard?' Sara said. She had already decided to take the flat if it turned out that she could afford it.

'All that flap between her and Mr Oliver.' The woman gave her a quick glance. 'You didn't hear it? I was sure you must've, coming in when you did.'

Sara shook her head. 'I didn't hear anything. But when

I rang a man opened the door and hurried out. Would that have been Mr Cannon?'

'Must've been. And there, I shouldn't have mentioned it, should I, except that I thought you'd have heard them at it and it might be worrying you? Perhaps the front door was closed for once. They leave it wide open half the time. Anyway, that sort of thing doesn't happen often, their shouting at each other like that, they're ever so attached to each other really. Some people would say too attached. I'm not sure it's healthy for a middle-aged man to be so fond of his mother.'

There was an eager light in Mrs Worth's grey eyes, the eagerness of the born gossip who has found a really splendid opportunity to have her say unchecked. She plunged on, 'After all, it's only natural for Mr Oliver to think of getting married, wouldn't you say? And I don't think that would upset Mrs Cannon so much if he hadn't got this idea of going to Canada into his head. I don't know where he's got this idea from. He's got a good job at the Agricultural College here. But I believe it's something to do with being a professor. But why it has to be Canada I don't really know. Have you ever been there, Mrs Marriott?'

'Once or twice, on holiday,' Sara answered. She had been taken to it by her mother and her stepfather in the days before she had married.

'But don't they have terribly cold winters?'

'Pretty cold, I believe, but I've only been there in the summers. Up in the mountains. It was very beautiful.'

'If it wasn't for the cold, Mrs Cannon could go with them, only she could never stand the cold, not at her age. Not that there's anything to be said for our climate, but we don't go in for extremes much, would you say? And I suppose that makes a difference when you're old. Anyway, she wouldn't like to leave Edgewater, not after all these years here. She's got her friends and her bridge and the church.

It would hardly be fair to expect her to give all that up. And then again, perhaps Miss Hancock wouldn't want her. I mean, it's only natural, isn't it, for a woman not to want to have her mother-in-law in the house right from the start when she first gets married? Later, of course, it might work, if they were fond of each other. But I can't help feeling that Miss Hancock and Mrs Cannon don't exactly . . . But what am I doing, talking like this? What I was meaning to say is, I can give you a morning a week, it you'd like me to. I did it for the last people and I know I can easily get round this little place in a couple of hours or less. Just tell Mrs Cannon if you'd like it and she can fix it up with me.'

Sara realized that Mrs Worth was under the impression that she had already taken the flat. Probably, Sara thought, she was right. If it turned out that the rent was what she could afford, it would suit her perfectly. But talking the matter over with Mrs Cannon a few minutes later and finding that the rent was considerably less than she had anticipated, she felt that she had to explain something.

'I don't really believe I shall be staying for three months,' she said. 'I don't know exactly what General Schofield expects or what he's told you, but I think we'll be working very hard together for some time, not very long, then I'll go home with my tape-recordings of all our talks and get to work there on the book. So it doesn't look as if I'm the tenant you want.'

She and the old woman were in the drawing-room again, Sara now the one who was standing and Mrs Cannon the one who was sitting in the chair by the window. Her pouting lips were pressed tightly together and she was frowning slightly.

'You like the flat, you said,' she said sharply. 'And you think the rent's reasonable.'

'Oh yes, indeed, but as I was saying—'

'Take it by the week, then,' Mrs Cannon interrupted.

'You're just the kind of tenant I want. You'll be quiet and careful and you won't give me any trouble. We won't bother about a lease. Just pay me by the week in advance, that will be perfectly satisfactory. And it isn't as if I've anyone else in view at the moment. I haven't even put a notice about it in the *Advertiser*. When would you like to move in?'

'If tomorrow's convenient.. . .'

'Yes, certainly tomorrow. Tomorrow morning? I don't suppose you've much luggage.'

'No, but I've a car.' Sara felt that she was being rushed off her feet before she had really had a chance to think out what she meant to do, but that it would probably be foolish to miss the opportunity that she was being offered.

'There's plenty of room in the garage unless you've brought a monster,' Mrs Cannon said. 'My son can show it to you when he gets in. So that's settled.'

She sprang to her feet and held out her hand. Her sudden smile had unexpected charm. Perhaps when she had been younger, when her plump face had been rosier and less creased into wrinkles, it had had considerable attraction.

'I'm sure we shall get on very well together,' she said.

Sara felt a bit less sure of this than it appeared that Mrs Cannon did. Remembering Mrs Worth's flow of information about her employers, it seemed to Sara that a household consisting of an apparently possessive mother and a son who had clung to her into middle age, then when she was old and vulnerable was trying to break away from her with a woman whom she did not even like and to go far away, might not be the most peaceful of locations. However, the little flat was self-contained and she would be spending most of her time in the quiet company of General Schofield.

With the key of the flat in her hand and having written a cheque for a week's rent, which indeed was very moderate, she returned for lunch at the Red Lion.

CHAPTER 2

When Sara had had lunch and had the rest of the day before her, it struck her that it would have been sensible to arrange with Mrs Cannon that she should bring her belongings over from the inn that afternoon. She might even have moved in that evening, then there would have been no problem next day about arriving punctually at ten o'clock to start work with General Schofield. As it was, if she was to move into the flat in the morning, she was almost certain to be late. In the circumstances it seemed best to telephone him to explain this. He sounded very pleased that she had made the arrangement that she had with Mrs Cannon, and said that he would not expect her until eleven o'clock. She did all the packing that she could in the afternoon, not that she had brought much with her, then went for a stroll through the little town, refreshing her memories of it.

Edgewater was in a valley between the South Downs and the Hampshire Downs. The low hills to the south were bare and green, those to the north covered with beechwoods. It was the wooded hills, with their rich treasures of spring flowers, that in the past had had a special attraction for Sara. There was one meadow at the foot of these where she could distinctly remember seeing primroses, violets, anenomes, lady's slipper, cuckoo flowers and wild orchids all blooming together in the grass. Because Granborough, the school at which she had been, had been a so-called progressive place, she and her friends had been allowed to roam the countryside in small bands and had been able to discover its beauties for themselves. That such a glory of blossom had been able to survive together must have meant bad farming, she supposed, and with an Agricultural College, new since her time, now in the neighbourhood, they had probably vanished under the stern onslaught of weedkiller. But the sight of them was something that she would never forget.

If it had been spring now, instead of August, she might have tried to find her way to that meadow, though the walk would have been longer than she contemplated, although she could not really remember the way there. And for all she knew, there might be a main road, heavy with traffic, cleaving its way through it. It was probably best to let the memory live on untested.

Yet she had been glad to leave school. She had been happy enough there as a young child, but had tired of it early and had persuaded her mother to let her have a year abroad before she went on to university. She had had six months in Paris and six in Vienna, had had one or two love-affairs in each, more or less pleasurable, then, almost reluctant to return to what at first had felt almost like more school work, she had gone to University College and there she had met Mark.

And how wonderful that had seemed, though not for very long. Now she could only think of it as a most bitter waste of her precious youth, though incidentally she had achieved a second-class degree, and then found work at which she was at least competent.

Next morning she packed her belongings into her car, a small Renault, and drove it the fifty yards or so from the garage of the Red Lion to that of her new lodging. The door of the house was standing open, but she rang the Cannons' bell and Oliver Cannon came out to greet her. He did not seem at all as she remembered him from yesterday. He had a pleasant smile, said that he hoped she was going to like the flat and that if it turned out that there was anything she needed she had only to let his mother know.

He showed her the garage, then carried her luggage upstairs for her. As it had been yesterday, the door of the flat was unlocked and she wondered if this was the custom of the house. It it was, she was quite happy to stick to it. She had brought no valuables with her. She had one suitcase, a typewriter and a tape-recorder. She wondered if the telephone had been disconnected since the last tenants had left, but found that it had not. After unpacking quickly, she made a few calls, one to her publisher to tell her editor that she was beginning work with General Schofield that day, and one or two to friends, giving them her new number. Then, switching on the answerphone, which she supposed the former tenants had left behind because they were going abroad, though she had no reason to expect any calls that morning, she set off up the High Street to General Schofield's house.

He let her in himself and took her into the square brown room where they had talked the day before. But he seemed fidgety and nervous and far less ready to talk then he had been then. Shy herself, Sara recognized the symptoms of the affliction and after they had sat together almost silent for some minutes, asked him if he would prefer her to turn the tape-recorder off until he had made up his mind what he wanted to say. Then she began to ask him a few simple questions about how it had happened that he had been born in Burma.

He began to talk more freely then about his parents and the importance to him throughout his childhood, even after he had been sent to England, of their connection with that far country. From that he wandered to childish memories of the First World War. He had been seven years old when it had broken out and what had impressed him most vividly, it seemed, of all that it had signified, had been the taste of the margarine that he had had to eat.

'Terrible stuff, you know,' he said, 'terrible. Quite different from what you can get nowadays. I found it so revolting that I wouldn't eat it. I preferred to have my plum and apple straight on dry bread. And then when the Second War came along and we had to eat margarine again, some memory of that old stuff made me refuse it. Anyone who liked could have my ration of it. And I took an oath—yes, it was almost a solemn oath—that I'd never eat margarine again. And nowadays, when they keep trying to persuade one that dairy products are bad for one, I think of that oath and I stick to butter. Only the real thing. I know if someone slipped me a pat of the stuff they make now and said it was butter, I might not know the difference, but to go into a shop and buy it with my eyes open, no . . . Only this isn't the sort of thing I ought to be talking about, is it? You know, my mother learnt to speak Burmese. She was very interested in the people, told me how the women always had flowers in their hair and how pretty they were and how they ran things. All quite different now, I believe. The war changed everything. That's what I remember of the country, of course, the Second War. I was taken prisoner and just how I came through that I'll never know. Mostly luck, of course. I saw many poor devils die . . .'

At some point while he had been talking Sara had un-obtrusively switched on her tape-recorder and though he had seen her do it, he had only smiled, as if this now rather pleased him, and had gone on chatting. At half past twelve he said he thought that that was enough for the present and once more offered her sherry.

They drank it together, then Sara said she ought to get out to the shops to buy some essential supplies and would like to spend the afternoon working on the material he had already given her, but she would appear next day at ten o'clock. She did her shopping in a supermarket in the High Street, buying bread, butter, eggs, tea, coffee, milk, cheese, apples and a frozen quiche which she thought would suit her for the evening, then returned to the flat and had a lunch of bread and cheese and coffee and began to think how she would handle the material that the General had given her.

She made several pages of notes before she began to see how she thought she would do this. After a little it began to seem to her that the time to begin was not in the happy and colourful days of his parents' life in Rangoon, but in the terrible days of the prison camp. Then she would jump backwards to the prosperous days of the Empire, to the life of many servants, of luxury and white dominance, but still of plague, cholera, typhoid, malaria and insufficient doctors. They had been brave people, the ones who had endured the side-effects of greatness. All too often there were early deaths. In the General's own family two children had died of some infection that was rife in the district up country to which his father had been sent. That had been partly why he himself had been sent to spend his childhood in his aunt's pleasant old house in the High Street of Edgewater.

But Sara needed far more material than she had yet acquired before making too definite a scheme of how to lay out the book, and her plan would have to be discussed with the General to see if it met with his approval. About five o'clock she put her papers away and went for a walk.

As she remembered it, there was something that was called the Heath on the edge of the town, a kind of park through which there meandered a placid, reed-bordered stream. She found her way to it without any difficulty and went strolling along beside the stream, finding the whole scene almost unchanged since she had seen it last, quietly green and peaceful, except that on the far side of the Heath where there had once been only a few scattered bungalows and rising beyond them the Downs, there was now a size-able, solid-looking concrete building with many large windows that reflected the August evening sun, and a straggle of outbuildings round it. She wondered if this was the Agricultural College where Oliver Cannon was employed.

For a little while she sat on a bench, watching some children throwing stones into the stream, trying to make them bounce along the surface of the water. Then she strolled back towards her flat, but before going into it she turned into the bar of the Red Lion and bought a bottle of Tio Pepe. She was just about to enter the door of the house opposite when she saw that the door of the flat in the basement was open and that a man was standing there, looking up at her. He looked a few years older than she was and was tall and strongly built, with thick, curly dark hair, a square, tanned face with dark eyes behind thick, dark-rimmed spectacles, and a wide, well-shaped mouth that showed excellent white teeth when he smiled, as he was doing now. He was wearing jeans, sandals and a not very clean white shirt.

'Hello,' he said, 'are you the new tenant?'

She admitted that she was.

'We're neighbours, then,' he said. 'I live down here. My name's Fryer. Paul Fryer. Unless you're in a hurry for some reason, you might perhaps consider joining me for a drink. We're all very friendly in this household.'

Sara rather liked the look of him. She said that her name was Sara Marriott and descended the steps to the doorway where he was standing. He showed her into the room into which it led. Because it had only one window and that was on a level below the street, it was not very well lit, but it was a pleasant room in a casual, shabby way. Everything in it looked as if it had had a busy, demanding, but on the whole well-loved life. The open bureau with a typewriter on its flap, with a heap of paper beside it, was probably Georgian. The carpet was worn but of soft, attractive colouring. Chairs were covered in a variety of somewhat faded materials that did not match. One wall was covered with bookcases. There was only one picture on the walls and that was a reproduction of Monet's irises. A room, she thought, in which someone who was probably intelligent and unpretentious was contented.

'You've been buying yourself Tio Pepe, so perhaps you might like some now,' he said as he closed the door behind them. 'Or would you like something stronger?'

'No, Tio Pepe would be fine,' she said. 'Have you lived here long?'

'About two years.' He disappeared into what she supposed was his kitchen and returned with a bottle and glasses. 'I work at a school called Granborough, just a little way out of the town. A bit of a queer place till you get used to it, but then it rather grows on you. Plenty of freedom for everybody, the staff included. I teach when I find enough children who seem to want me to, or sometimes just if I happen to feel like it. It's really very interesting. Not that I believe your schooling has much effect on you in the end. You turn into what you were always meant to be.'

'I was at Granborough myself,' Sara said as she sat down in a chair covered in a worn green tweedy material. He brought her drink to her and put it down on a low table beside her. 'I remember being very happy there when I was a young child, then getting rather bored with it and insisting on being sent abroad where every moment of my day was strictly organized and I really found that as interesting as all that freedom. Anyway, it was a new experience. What do you teach?'

'Biology.' He sat down on a sofa that looked as if perhaps some of its springs were broken. 'And you've come to a job at the Agricultural College, have you?'

'Oh no, I'm just a sort of hack writer,' Sara said. 'I'm helping a very nice old General write his memoirs.'

'Ah, I think I've heard about that. He's a friend of Mrs Cannon's, isn't he?'

'Yes, it was he who sent me here with a recommendation to her as a suitable sort of tenant. But what are you doing here in the middle of August? The school's on holiday, isn't it?'

'Yes, but I thought I could use the time quite profitably at home. I'm a sort of writer too. I write thrillers. Actually I'm on my third, so I'm beginning to feel almost professional. Not that one can keep up for thrills with what one can watch on the news every evening. If I littered my pages with as many bodies as we're used to being told have been found night after night in every country from Ireland to South Africa, I believe I'd be told it was too improbable. Life's very improbable at the moment, isn't it?'

'We certainly seem to be going through a very strange phase of history,' she agreed. 'One grew up with the idea of wars being the worst things possible, but now that sometimes seems like a peaceful old dream. What's happening round us now is just a bloody, bestial horror. But if you're writing thrillers, do you really find Edgewater a stimulating place to stay? Isn't life here too quiet, too good-mannered, too safe?'

'But it's just that that suits me,' he said. 'I can let my imagination run riot and there are no uncomfortable facts to contradict me. All the same, in the end I may have to stick to biology. When I was young I wanted to be a farmer, but luckily it dawned on me in time that for that you have to have capital. Mrs Cannon has a nephew who's a farmer. His farm's quite near here. Have you met him yet? They've got children at Granborough.'

She shook her head. 'I've met her son very briefly. He works at the Agricultural College, doesn't he?'

'Yes, he's an agricultural economist. He's working there for the present. But there's a rumour that he's thinking of taking off for Canada. I don't know what it'll do to the old lady if he goes. It'll be about as tough on her as losing a husband. Which reminds me, haven't you a husband somewhere? What does he do?'

She did not answer and after a moment he said, 'I'm sorry, that's plainly one the things that shouldn't have been said.'

She smiled. 'It's just that I'm still not used to talking about it, but I've got to learn to do it. He's in publishing as it happens, but we split up. Are you married?'

'No.'

'And never have been?'

'No.'

'Do you think there are any other vital things we ought to know about one another if we're going to be neighbours?'

'I believe you're annoyed with me for asking what I did,' he said.

'Only a little bit. And I ought to be going. Thank you for the drink. You must come up and have one with me one day.'

He said that he would look forward to it and saw her out to the street.

As usual, the front door of the house was open and she went in and climbed the long staircases to her flat, made sure that no message had been left for her on the answerphone, poured herself out another glass of sherry, then settled down to watch the six o'clock news.

It was much as usual and what with murders in Northern Ireland, civil wars in Africa, thousands dying of starvation in Ethiopia and a coup in South America, it seemed to her that her neighbour, Paul Fryer, had been right when he had said that the mere writer of thrillers, even if he had a murder per page, had very little chance of competing with reality. Presently she cooked the quiche that she had bought in the morning, made coffee, read for a time of the golden world of Trollope and went early to bed.

For the next few days she worked quietly with General Schofield, arriving at his house punctually at ten o'clock, encouraging him to talk freely to her tape-recorder, discussing with him the lay-out of his book, and showing him portions of what she was making of his rambling chatter, which, she could tell, he was coming to enjoy more and more as he went on. She saw very little of Mrs Cannon or her son. Sometimes they passed in the small front hall of the house and exchanged remarks about the weather. Once Mrs Worth appeared at her door before she set out and asked her if she would like her to clean the flat and Sara thankfully assured her that she would be delighted if she would go ahead, paid her and left her in charge. She took to having her lunch in a small café called the Green Tree Café and only cooked a snack for herself in the evenings. General Schofield wanted to know if she was quite happy.

'Oh, I think I've been so lucky, finding that flat,' she said. 'I'm so grateful to you for sending me to it.'

'And you get on all right with Althea Cannon, do you?' he asked.

'To tell you the truth, I've hardly seen her,' she said.

'I'm very fond of her, you know, always have been,' he said, 'but I know she can be difficult. Very emotional woman. Very moody. Been all wrapped up in that son of hers since her husband died. I sometimes think life hasn't been too easy for him, though I must say I admire the way he's looked after her. There's talk now that he wants to get married but that the girl won't agree to it unless he cuts loose from Althea and goes off abroad. Tough position for him. I heard all about it from a niece of Althea's, married to a farmer, a very nice fellow. But if she's right, you know, and Oliver gets married and leaves his mother, it'll just about break her heart. Not that parents' hearts aren't made to be broken, one way or another, but it usually happens to them when they're younger and tougher.'

That was the day when Sara, returning to the flat to deposit the tape-recorder and her notes before setting out for her lunch in the café, met Mrs Cannon in the doorway of her apartment and was commanded with a frowning sort of assertiveness to come into it for a drink. Her cheeks were as flushed as they had been when Sara had first met her and her dark eyes were blazing.

'Would you believe it,' the old woman cried in her shrill, harsh voice as she led Sara into the drawing-room, 'today is my eightieth birthday and nobody—but nobody—has taken the slightest notice of it!'

Sara did not think that Mrs Cannon had been speaking the truth. Spread out on a table were a number of objects that had not been removed from colourful wrapping paper, of the kind only used for presents. There were also more flowers in the room than she remembered seeing there before, some in carefully arranged bowls and decorated with pink ribbons.

Mrs Cannon saw her looking at them.

'Presents!' she said scornfully. 'Of course they all sent me presents. They always do. Chocolates which I never eat. A scarf that doesn't go with anything I've got to wear. A bottle of scent which it would be utterly ridiculous to use at my age. No, what I thought there'd be is some kind of celebration. After all, an eightieth birthday is an eightieth birthday. I thought the family would get together and we'd probably have champagne and even one or two speeches, very short speeches, of course, because naturally it would be very informal, but still I thought for sure we'd have a party. I was so sure of it that I was always very careful not to say a word about it, because I knew they'd mean it to be a surprise for me and I didn't want to spoil it for them by letting them know I'd been expecting it. And what's really happening? Nothing! Isn't it natural to feel upset? Now what would you like to drink? I'm drinking Campari soda, it's what I always drink in hot weather like this, but I've got most of the other things.'

Sara said that she would like Campari soda. She sat down in the chair near the window and Mrs Cannon brought her her drink.

'Well,' she said in a rather challenging way, as if she felt that there was something that Sara should already have said to her, 'how do you like it here? Are you comfortable?'

'Very,' Sara said. 'I'm so grateful to you for letting me have the flat, even though I probably won't be staying nearly three months.'

'It seemed to me you looked the kind of person who wouldn't be any trouble,' Mrs Cannon said, 'and there was no point in letting the place stay empty, even for a short while. Tenants can be a fearful bother, though on the whole I've been lucky with them. Oliver warned me when I decided to have the house converted that I'd regret it. He wanted me to sell it and move into one of those new small houses on the edge of town. But I've lived here ever since my marriage, and on the whole things have worked out very well. I make up my mind very quickly about people and I haven't made many mistakes. I had my doubts at first about the man who's been living in the basement. Have you met him? His name's Fryer. I thought he might be inclined to give rowdy parties and play pop music and let everything get into a disgusting mess, but I was quite wrong. As it's turned out, he's one of the best tenants I've ever had, always ready to do bits of shopping for me and to do odd jobs, like changing electric light bulbs, which is the sort of thing Oliver hates doing, and he once even decorated a room for me, free of charge. Said he enjoyed doing it, it gave him time to think. Of course he teaches at that

crazy school, Granborough, and I think they collect some
pretty strange specimens there, but Paul Fryer and I have
become the best of friends.'

'I was at Granborough myself for a time,' Sara said.

'You were?' The little woman gave her a searching stare.
'I'd never have thought it. You seem to me quite normal.'

'I think in the end they all turn out pretty normal,' Sara
said.

'I hope so, I hope so. A grand-niece and grand-nephew
of mine are there at the moment and I must admit they
seem a very nice pair of children. Twins, you know, but not
identicals. A boy and a girl. Their mother is a niece of mine
and she's married to a farmer. Their farm is only about five
miles from Edgewater, and that's very nice for me, because
we see quite a lot of one another. And if certain things
happen, which I keep being told are going to happen, it'll
turn out very nice for them too. I'm not a very rich woman.
I haven't a great deal to leave them, but it'll certainly make
them comfortable if, as I now intend, I leave it all to my
niece instead of to that selfish son of mine who's thought
all his life he could count on it, however he treated me. My
mind's made up and that's such a relief. I'm seeing my
solicitor tomorrow and making a new will. I've told them
all so. My niece Meg will inherit everything I've got and
my dear son will get absolutely nothing. I wonder if his
beloved Celia will be quite as keen on marrying him when
she knows that.'

Sara's reaction to the flow of information was profound
embarrassment. She did not in the least want to know how
Mrs Cannon intended to leave her money. Remembering
that when she had first met her, the old woman had claimed
to be in a state of shock but at least to have made up her
mind about something, it seemed to Sara probable that that
had been the time when Mrs Cannon had learnt definitely
that her son was marrying and was leaving her and that

she had decided to disinherit him. But what had that to do with Sara? Only one thing about it seemed important to her and that was that she should not be drawn into taking sides.

'Anyway, whichever of them you leave it to,' she said, 'they'll probably have to wait years for it.'

'Oh, of course, you'd be bound to say that,' Mrs Cannon said. 'The official theory is that I shall live for ever, while behind their hands they all whisper about how tired and old I'm looking, and so on. But Meg and Ron—that's her husband—will really be very glad of anything I can do for them. Granborough's an expensive place. I wanted them to send their children to more conventional schools, but they insisted on a coeducational boarding school, progress-ive and all that, so that the twins needn't be split up, and then they wanted them somewhere near at hand. Ron dotes on them, you know, and even though they're boarders at Granborough, he can see them at weekends and go and watch them when they're acting in plays or playing in matches. Personally I think it's healthier for twins to be split up so that they don't grow up too dependent on one another, but Ron wouldn't hear of it. Poor Meg, I some-times think she's a bit jealous because he cares for them so much, but then she's got her art to keep her occupied, and for all I know, Ron's jealous of that. She's a sculptor, you know, but I don't believe she's made much of a name for herself. Oh dear, family relationships are really very diffi-cult things, aren't they? If only they were all children still! Things used to be so easy in those days. My friend, General Schofield, has told me that my trouble is I've tried to keep them all children, but I'm sure that isn't true. I'm not like that at all.'

During the last few days Sara had been developing a feeling that General Schofield had a great deal of good sense besides the courtesy and kindliness that he invariably showed, and here in what he had said to Mrs Cannon she felt fairly sure he had been right, even though Mrs Cannon herself would probably assert, if she were pressed, that she never dreamt of interfering with anyone. She and Sara chatted for a few minutes more, then Sara finished her Campari soda, wished Mrs Cannon many happy returns of the day, and went up to her flat.

The red light on the answerphone was on as she entered, telling her that someone had rung up while she had been out and had left a message. But when she listened to what was on the tape a sense of complete bewilderment took possession of her. The voice that she heard was a woman's and unfamiliar to her.

It said, 'Darling, it's me . . . Yes, I thought you'd know . . . It's really all right then about the party, is it? . . . Everything organized? . . . Oh, I'm so glad, but you're sure it's all right for me to come? . . . I sometimes think she doesn't like me much . . . Oh yes, I do want to be there and if you feel really sure she'd like to have me . . . That's fine then, I'll be there at six o'clock. I do so admire her, you know, and feel sorry for her and just so long as she won't feel I'm intruding . . . I'll see you there, then. Lots of love, meanwhile.'

The message ended.

Sara stared at the machine in disbelief, then played the tape again. There had been no mistake. The second time was exactly the same as the first. But since when had answerphones been able to conduct conversations? For that was what it sounded like. It sounded as if someone had been talking into a telephone and while what she said had been recorded on Sara's tape, someone else had been answering her, telling her something about the arrangements for a party. But answerphones do not answer back. Or had there recently been some miraculous advance in technology that would make this possible? Could this house be wired in such a way that someone not in this flat had been able to receive this message and to reply to it, while the one voice only had been recorded here?

Sara was ready to believe almost anything of modern technology. She had never been in the least mechanically minded. She could be easily baffled by what could and could not be achieved. All the same, she did not believe in answerphones that answered back. Someone had been playing a joke with hers, pretending to be holding a conversation with someone who of course was not there.

Why the owner of the unknown feminine voice should have done such a thing she could not guess. Then she remembered that Mrs Cannon had told her that she had a grand-niece and and a grand-nephew and that they were children. She had not mentioned their ages, but it did seem possible that a ten- or eleven-year-old child might think it amusing to hold what would have sounded to someone who overheard it like a rather sophisticated sort of conversation with some imaginary character. But had the voice sounded like a child's? It had sounded young, but not, as Sara recalled it, actually childish. She played it a third time and thought that it just could be either a young girl's or a boy's, if his had not yet broken, particularly if they were given to imitating the voices of the grown-ups they knew. Anyway, it had certainly been someone amusing herself in an odd but harmless way.

She left her tape-recorder and her notes in the flat and went out to the Green Tree Café for her lunch.

She had a visitor that afternoon. At three o'clock her doorbell rang and when she opened the door she heard heavy footsteps mounting the stairs. A moment later Oliver Cannon appeared. He paused when he saw her above him, then climbed the rest of the way up to the top storey.

'Are you busy?' he asked. 'Am I interrupting anything?'

'No,' she said, although in fact she had been hard at work

on a portion of the General's story when he had been at Sandhurst. 'Come in.'

He entered the room and she closed the door behind him. He stood still in the middle of the room, looking round him.

'I haven't been up here for some time,' he said. 'It looks different somehow.'

'Perhaps the people who used to live here were tidier than I am,' she suggested. 'Do sit down.'

He chose a chair beside the unlit electric fire and she sat down on one facing him. The only changes in the room since she had seen it first were that her typewriter was on a table, a number of papers were scattered about and a big bunch of gladioli from General Schofield's small garden, which he had picked for her that morning, was in a vase that she had found in a cupboard.

'I hope you're quite comfortable here,' Oliver Cannon said. His big, heavy-featured face looked pleasantly friendly. 'You come and go so quietly we'd never know there was anyone here if Mrs Worth didn't say she sometimes sees you.'

'She cleaned the flat for me the other day,' Sara said, 'for which I was very grateful.'

'Oh, she's a splendid worker and quite reliable,' he answered, 'but if there are any dark secrets in your life, I'd advise you to keep them very carefully hidden, or my mother and I will know all about them. I'm sure she's told you all kinds of things about us.'

She wondered if he was trying to find out if Mrs Worth had actually told her about his possible marriage, or if perhaps he was simply warning her that letters which she was at all afraid of having read should not be left lying about.

She chose what she thought was safe ground. 'She told me she thought you were thinking of going to a job in Canada.'

His lips twitched a little as if he were holding back some retort. But then he said casually, 'It's true, I might be. I'm rather tempted. I've lived nearly all my life in Edgewater, except for the time I was at Cambridge. But what I really came up here to ask you is whether you'd feel like coming to a small party we're giving for my mother this evening. It's a surprise party. It's her eightieth birthday and we've collected a few people to drop in for drinks. When I say we, I mean my cousin Meg and her family. Actually it was Meg's idea and she'll run the show. I'm not much good when it comes to parties. Of course General Schofield will be there, and Paul Fryer—he's the tenant in the basement, I don't know if you've met him yet—and one or two other people. We've got some champagne and Meg's going to bring some of those little bits and pieces you have to offer people at parties, and I believe we've managed to keep it absolutely secret. I don't think my mother has the least suspicion that it's going to happen.'

'She's got so little suspicion of it that she's actually feeling very hurt because you're doing nothing,' Sara said. 'Did you know that?'

'Good lord, no, is she really?' He looked dismayed. 'We never thought of that. You mean she's been expecting a celebration of some sort and is feeling horribly let down because it seems nothing's happening? That's really a pity. I'm afraid surprises often have a way of going wrong. We ought to have thought of that. You think a hint of mystery in the air, as if there were some secret we were carefully keeping from her, would have cheered her up?'

'I believe it would have been more tactful.'

'Of course you're right. And now it's too late to do any-thing about it. She'll just have to wait for the party to happen. That'll cheer her up anyway, won't it? She's having her usual rest now, so I won't disturb her to start dropping hints. But will you come?'

'Thank you very much,' Sara said. 'I should love to.'

'It'll be very small and quite informal. Just the family and one or two friends, as I said. And come about six o'clock.'

He stood up, about to leave, when Sara said, 'Oh, Mr Cannon . . .'

'Oliver,' he suggested.

'Oliver,' she said. 'I was going to ask you . . .' But there she paused, for reminded of it by his talk of a party that was to start at six o'clock, she had been about to tell him of the strange message left on her answerphone which had had something to do with such a party, and to ask him if he could explain it. But just before doing so an idea had occurred to her, an idea so preposterous, so ridiculous, so melodramatic, that she knew that if she were to mention it, it would merely make her look a fool. And yet somehow it seemed just possible that it made sense of the message. She changed what she had been about to say and only asked, 'Who were the people who lived in this flat before me?'

'Their name was Marsden,' he answered. 'A young couple, Sam and Harriet Marsden. I didn't know them well. He worked for a building society, I believe, and they left because he'd got a job in New Zealand.'

'So that's why they left their answerphone behind. I suppose it wouldn't have been much use taking it with them. How long were they here?'

'About three years, I think. Why? Is there anything the matter?'

'Oh no, nothing at all. I was just curious about them, I'm not sure why.' She knew that it sounded stupid, but not as stupid as what she really had in her mind would have sounded if she had tried to tell him about it.

'So you'll come about six o'clock,' Oliver Cannon said as he went to the door. 'Don't forget.'

'I'll look forward to it,' Sara answered.

CHAPTER 3

She was not speaking quite the truth. Parties at which there would be no one whom she knew scared her as much as they attracted her. She could never think of what is was possible to talk about to strangers and she always felt that no one could want to talk to her. It was true that she had a slight knowledge of the two Cannons and of Paul Fryer, and of course of General Schofield, and that might help, and she supposed that she ought to feel pleased that she had been invited. But she knew that she would be very glad when it was over.

A minor embarrassment was that when she had packed her suitcase to come to Edgewater, she had not dreamt that there would be any question of parties, and she had not brought any dress with her that seemed proper for one. It was the kind of thing that worried her. However, Oliver Cannon had insisted that the occasion was to be informal, so a cotton dress that she had brought would have to do. She had her gold earrings and some coral beads. At a few minutes after six o'clock she went downstairs to the Cannons' apartment.

Everything was mysteriously quiet. Was that because she was arriving too punctually, she wondered. Then she found that the door was open and that a number of people were already collected in the drawing-room. But they were all being very careful to move about quietly and were talking in whispers. After a moment of bewilderment she realized what was happening. This was the surprise party for Mrs Cannon. She was not to know anything about the assembling of her guests until she walked into the room and found them collected there already, possibly about to burst into song. 'Happy birthday to you . . .'

She was not there yet. Her afternoon rest appeared to be a lengthy one.

Seeing Sara come in, Oliver Cannon came towards her and said in a low voice, 'Come and meet my cousin. I told you she was really running the show. Meg—' he turned to a young woman who was standing talking quietly to the General—'this is Sara. Sara Marriott, our new tenant upstairs. Sara, this is Meg Kimberley.'

Meg Kimberley looked if she were about thirty-five years old. She was a tall, slender woman with straight dark hair cut in a heavy fringe across her forehead and docked short behind her small, well-shaped head. Her eyes were large, dark and intense. She was in black slacks and a frilly black and white blouse and had long, red plastic earrings hanging from her ears.

'We've been told that you're the perfect tenant,' Meg whispered to her. 'My aunt has taken a tremendous fancy to you.'

'All my doing,' General Schofield said, joining in the low-pitched conversation. 'I sent her here. I knew I couldn't be wrong.'

'Mum,' a young boy said in an almost normal tone of voice and was immediately shushed. He dropped his voice. 'Sorry, I forgot. Mum, can I have one of these mushroom things?'

On a table, besides glasses, a number of dishes had been set out filled with what looked like very tempting snacks, small triangles of bread covered with smoked salmon, little tartlets filled with black lumpfish roe, fluffy-looking patties filled with mushrooms and creamy-looking seafood, all plainly very appealing to a boy of twelve or thereabouts. He was not in the least like his mother. His hair was fair and his eyes were blue and his face was square and rosy. He was dressed in jeans and a T-shirt.

'No, Nick, wait until Aunt Althea comes down,' Meg Kimberley said. 'Then you can have some champagne as well.'

'Well, I wish she'd come,' Nick said. 'You know, I wouldn't be at all surprised if she knows we're all here and is keeping us waiting on purpose. It'd be just like her.'

This thought had crossed Sara's mind. It seemed to her possible that Mrs Cannon, by prolonging her normal rest, was taking a small revenge on her family for their apparent neglect of her birthday. She was now going to do what she could to spoil the occasion for them.

A man of about Meg's age, joining the group, observed, 'If she does know we're here, I think I know what she's doing. She's dressing herself up in the most gorgeous dress she's got and putting on her most precious jewellery, just to show us that that's how we all ought to have got ourselves up.'

He himself was in cotton trousers and an open-necked shirt and had his sleeves rolled up, showing powerful arms covered with pale golden hair. His hair was fair and his eyes were blue and he had a square face, deeply tanned. In fact, he bore a noticeable likeness to the boy who had wanted a mushroom patty.

'This is my husband, Ron,' Meg said to Sara. 'Ron, this is Sara Marriott, who's taken the flat upstairs. Jill, Jill, what do you think you're doing?' She had turned towards the table on which the plates and glasses were set out and for a moment had let her voice rise before recollecting that this was something that she must not do, and her question ended in a harsh whisper.

Jill, to whom it had been addressed, had just popped one of the triangles of bread topped with smoked salmon into her mouth. She was obviously the twin of Nick, fair-haired, blue-eyed and square-faced like him, the same age and about the same height and, like him, she was in jeans and a T-shirt. The main difference between them seemed to be that she helped herself to what she wanted without waiting to ask permission.

'You shouldn't have done that,' Meg said. 'I told you you were to wait.'

'For God's sake, Meg,' the children's father said, 'it doesn't matter so long as they don't actually eat everything up. Aunt Althea isn't going to go round counting what's left on all the plates.'

'But I told them we were all going to wait,' Meg said. 'They ought to have waited.'

'Well, this isn't the time and place to have a row about a scrap of smoked salmon,' he said.

'Oh, you always spoil them.' She sounded remarkably disturbed by the incident. 'And with that place Granborough you're so mad about teaching them always to do just whatever they like, it wouldn't surprise me if it soon turns out that they like smoking and drugs and God knows what else.'

'Granborough isn't at all like that,' the boy Nick said rather stiffly. 'Is it, Paul?'

He turned to Paul Fryer, who was talking to two young women near the window. He had apparently not heard the beginning of the argument and coming towards the group in the middle of the room said apologetically, 'Is it what, Nick?'

'Mum says Granborough's the sort of place where we all go in for drugs and sex and so on,' Nick said, 'but I said it isn't.'

'Nick, I didn't say that,' Meg said. 'I only said they let you have your own way about far too many things.'

'Paul doesn't think so,' Jill said. She helped herself to a biscuit spread with pâté. 'If he did he wouldn't teach there.

He's really very strict. He keeps telling us off if he thinks we're rude and he's ever so fussy about our language.'

'It's just that most bad language shows a terrible lack of imagination,' Paul said. 'There are very few words left that really shock people, whereas there are hundreds that don't which you can use to say what you really mean.'

'Then haven't those books you've written got any shits and fucks and sods and buggers in them?' Jill asked. 'No wonder they don't sell.'

'Who told you that?' Paul said.

'Oh, it's just that words like that are in everything one reads nowadays, so I suppose it's necessary,' she answered. 'I once read a book—'

'Jill,' the General interrupted, 'I don't know where you get your reading matter, but to us old folks those words lost their meaning a long time ago. They don't impress us.'

'Of course, she's just showing off,' Meg said. 'It's mere stupidity.'

'It's all right, she'll grow out of it,' Ron said.

'There you go again,' his wife said. 'You always back them up whatever they do. I think it's a fearful mistake. I don't believe in being specially strict, but I think all this liberty thing has gone a lot too far and we'll be sorry for it later.'

'When the illegitimate babies start arriving and so on,' he suggested.

'Ron!' she exclaimed angrily. 'You really shouldn't say things like that in front of them.'

'I only wish someone had talked a bit more like it when I was their age,' he muttered with a sound of sullenness. 'The amount of misinformation I acquired is perfectly astonishing to look back on and it's a painful business discovering how you've been kidded.'

'But we aren't all obsessed with sex and sniffing glue and so on at Granborough, are we, Paul?' Jill slid an arm under one of Paul Fryer's. 'We're mad keen on cricket, aren't we, and we go hiking for miles, and when we stop for a drink at a pub and one of the seniors goes in to order for us we only have ginger pop, and we read Dickens from beginning to end! I've just finished *A Tale of Two Cities*. It's fabulous! And there isn't a single bad word in it. But then, of course, he was a Victorian.'

'And knew a bit about how to write,' Paul murmured.

Sara was trying to remember how the children of her own generation at Granborough had addressed their teachers. She did not think it had been by their Christian names. She recalled a joke that had been current at one time there that they called the masters 'sir', and the mistresses 'please'. But her attention had wandered from the argument about education to the two young women whom Paul Fryer had left standing by the window, talking in soft-voiced conversation.

They were both about her own age, or so she guessed, though one, who was the smaller, the slightly plumper and in her way the prettier, might have been younger. She had a round, pink, dimpled face and hair which was obviously a natural silvery blonde and very curly. She had wide grey eyes that looked more innocent than Jill's and possibly rather stupid, a wide, soft mouth and a small firm chin. She was wearing a long full skirt with a flowery pattern on it, a sleeveless and almost backless black blouse and some colourful plastic bracelets.

Her companion had a more mature sort of solidity, fairly slim but firmly built, with straight brown hair drawn back from her face and tied in a pony-tail, a face that was almost triangular, with wide-spread brown eyes and a small mouth that oddly seemed to have a downward curve when she smiled. She was wearing a neat dark blue shirt and dark blue trousers.

It was she who noticed that Sara was looking at the two

of them and who advanced towards her, holding out a hand.

'I'm Celia Hancock,' she said, 'and I believe you're Mrs Marriott, the new tenant who's taken the flat the Marsdens had. And this is Kay Eldridge.' She drew the other young woman forward. 'Kay and I both work at the Agricultural College. Oliver's told us you're an authoress.'

Sara believed that Hancock was the name of the woman who Mrs Worth had told her was probably going to marry Oliver Cannon and between whom and Mrs Cannon there was no love lost. But at least if that were so the antagonism did not go so deep that she was unacceptable at an eightieth birthday party.

'I don't call myself a real authoress,' Sara said. 'I'm just helping to edit General Schofield's memoirs. I'm finding it very interesting, and he's got such extraordinary charm.'

Celia Hancock gave a glance at the old man.

'Just think what he must have been like when he was young,' she said with a laugh. 'Oliver's told me there was a time when he used to expect him and his mother to get married. He'd lost his wife and she'd lost her husband and they'd known each other for years. But the old boy was too shrewd to get hooked, though I doubt if it was for want of trying on her part. I've always admired Mrs Cannon, but I think it's best to do that from a slight distance.'

'For instance, from Canada,' Kay Eldridge said, in a husky whisper. She chuckled. She was studying Sara intently, almost as if she might in some way be important to her. Her eyes, after all, Sara thought, were not stupid, but merely bulged a little, which helped to give her, with her plump cheeks and softly resilient-looking body, a little the look of an over-sized and over-indulged Pekingese. 'Are you staying long?'

It had begun to seem to Sara that really Mrs Cannon might have been fortunate to avoid her eightieth birthday party. No one who had come to it had shown any sign of feeling much affection for her. Meg Kimberley, it was true, had so far had nothing to say against her, but Ron, her husband, had spoken of her mockingly and only too evidently neither of these two guests had any regard for her. Sara found herself taking Mrs Cannon's side against them, although until then she had not felt particularly drawn to the old woman.

'That depends on General Schofield,' she said, 'and perhaps on whether Mrs Cannon can find a tenant who'll want the place for a longer time than I shall. I'm just a stop-gap. It's very good of her to let me have the flat at all.'

Paul Fryer joined them. 'Isn't the old lady rather overdoing things?' he said. 'She must know there's something going on here by now.'

'Oh, any minute now she'll make a grand entrance,' Celia Hancock said, 'and be so surprised to see us all. I expect she's known all day this was going to happen.'

'I really don't think she did,' Sara said. 'When I saw her before lunch she seemed very upset that there weren't any signs of a celebration.'

'You saw her before lunch?' Kay Eldridge said, sounding curiously interested by the information. 'Where was that?'

'Why, here,' Sara answered. 'She asked me in for a drink and told me how disappointed she was.'

'You didn't have lunch with her?'

'Oh no, I went to the Green Tree Café. I generally go there for my lunch.'

'I see.'

It sounded as if this were important to Kay, though Sara could not understand what it was that Kay thought she saw.

'It's very pleasant there, and the food's pretty good, and it isn't expensive,' Sara said.

'Jill! Jill!' Forgetting to keep her voice down, Meg Kimberley sounded angry and excited. 'You are not to eat up all those things before Aunt Althea gets here! Haven't I told you that already?'

'But, darling, they're so delicious, I can't resist them.' The child spoke in a thin, high affected voice, an obvious parody of some adult, and then helped herself to a patty. 'Gorgeous!' she added in her own natural voice, licking her fingers. 'These are the best, Nick. Come on, have one.'

But in that moment when she had spoken in an artificial voice something had clicked in Sara's mind. Wasn't that the voice she had heard on her answerphone? So her first guess about that had been right. The strange message that had been left on it had simply been from a child, playing some little game of her own. The dark suspicion that had come later and lingered at the back of her mind was shown up as being just as absurd as in her heart she had known all along that it must be.

She was interested by the difference in the two children. Though they looked so alike, Jill had far the stronger personality, was the most self-assertive, the more sure of herself. Sara had a feeling that she was her father's favourite, though he now took hold of her by the arm and drew her away from the table where the good things were spread out.

'Greedy thing,' he said affectionately. 'Anyone would think your mother starved you while you were in London today.'

'Oh, have they been to London?' General Schofield asked.

'Yes, I took them up,' Meg answered. 'They wanted to buy something special for Aunt Althea, but you know how impossible it is to guess what she's going to like. They ended up buying something they'd like themselves.'

'So that if she doesn't like it, we can enjoy it,' Jill said. 'We got it at Fortnum's and it was fearfully expensive. But as she's going to leave all her money to Mum, we thought we ought to show that we appreciated it.'

'And what was it?' Paul Fryer asked.

'A great big pot of caviar,' Jill said. 'Real Russian caviar, not like this black stuff here. But I've never tasted caviar, and I thought I'd like to before I got much older.'

'We also got her a lovely silk scarf at Liberty's,' Meg said. 'That's what I hope she'll really like, but it's always very difficult, choosing things for her.'

'But she's really going to leave all her money to Mum,' Nick said. 'We'll be ever so rich some day. Can you really believe it?'

'Oh, I believe it,' Oliver said with a crooked smile. 'She's made that very plain to me. Our solicitor's coming to see her tomorrow. I made the appointment for that myself and she left me in no doubt about why she wanted to see him.'

'But why doesn't she come down?' General Schofield said. 'Do you think perhaps someone ought to go up and find out what's keeping her?'

'Yes,' Oliver said, 'I'll go.'

'No, let the children go,' Meg said. 'Nick and Jill, run upstairs and tell Aunt Althea we're all here waiting for her. But be nice about it, won't you? Be polite and nice.'

'The way you nag those children!' Ron muttered.

'Oh, we'll be ever so polite,' Jill said cheerfully. 'Nick will bow and I will curtsey and we'll both say, "Your Royal Highness, we await your pleasure."'

They ran together out of the room.

A short silence followed their departure, then Oliver said, 'We ought to start operating on the champagne, I suppose. Ron, are you any good at it? It isn't one of my gifts. When I try, corks fly all over the room.'

'I'll do it, if you like,' the General said. 'I'm out of practice, but I used to be quite proficient.'

The door burst open again. The children stood there, side by side, silent and white-faced.

Then Nick said, 'She's asleep. Or something. We can't make her wake up.'

Oliver rushed out of the room. Meg and Ron followed him. In the drawing-room there was silence, with only the sound of footsteps in the room overhead to be heard. The telephone gave a little tinkle, telling that an extension there had been lifted and after a minute or two there was another tinkle which told that it had been replaced. Jill and Nick had come into the room. They went as it seemed as a matter of course to the General, who put a hand on the shoulder of each. Their faces were solemn and apprehensive. A minute or two later Ron appeared at the door.

'A stroke,' he said. 'That's what it looks like. Poor old thing. And here were we, making jokes about her not joining us.'

'She's unconscious?' the General asked.

'Yes,' Ron said.

'But not . . . ?' The old man hesitated.

'Dead?' Ron said. 'No, she's breathing, but her pulse is very weak. Oliver's phoned for Stamforth. He'll be round in a few minutes.'

Sara presumed that Stamforth was a doctor.

'I wonder how long ago it happened,' General Schofield said.

'Perhaps Stamforth will be able to tell,' Ron answered. 'She's lying on her bed in a dressing-gown and there's a tray with her coffee on the table beside her. She usually had that when Mrs Worth had got her lunch and left. Mrs Worth would clear away the lunch and put it in the dishwasher and go and Aunt Althea would make herself some coffee—real coffee, not instant—and take it upstairs with her and lie down and drink it and read till she went off to sleep. And the coffee's been drunk and the book—it's Graham Greene—is lying on the floor by the bed, as if it had dropped there when she fell asleep. But in the normal way she'd have got up at least by half past four and come down to get herself some tea. I suppose we were very stupid, not realizing that something must be wrong when she wasn't here when we started arriving.'

'I think we all took for granted she knew about the party and was deliberately keeping out of the way so that she could really seem to have been taken by surprise,' the General said. 'But you're quite right, it was stupid of us.'

'I wonder if it would have made any difference,' Celia Hancock said, 'though perhaps getting her to hospital sooner might have helped. Dr Stamforth will send for an ambulance, I suppose.'

In fact it was what Dr Stamforth did a minute or two after his arrival. He was a youngish man, tall and spare, with a shock of hair going grey before its time and thick spectacles. He had a brisk, impersonal manner, though something about the way that he spoke to Oliver, with whom he came down to the drawing-room after some time spent in the bedroom upstairs, gave the impression that they knew each other well. Meg had remained with her aunt in the bedroom.

'I'm sorry I can't give you much hope,' the doctor said. 'At her age, and with her not very good health, there's still a chance that she'll pull round, but I wouldn't expect too much. I've given her an injection, but there's not much I can do myself at the moment.'

'Was it a stroke?' the General asked.

'It looks like it, but as a matter of fact . . .' The doctor paused.

'Yes?' the General said.

'There's something about it that's a bit peculiar,' Dr Stamforth replied. 'Did any of you see her earlier today?'

'I did, naturally, at breakfast,' Oliver said. His heavy

face had the blankness of great anxiety on it and was very pale. 'Why?'

'You didn't have lunch with her?'

'No.'

'And she was alone all day?'

'Except for Mrs Worth, who was here as usual in the morning and would have seen her when she served her lunch.'

'As a matter of fact,' Sara said, 'I saw her for a short time before she had her lunch. She asked me in for a drink.'

The doctor turned his cool, impersonal gaze on her and said, 'Ah!'

She thought that that was all that he was going to say and after a moment, like Oliver, she asked, 'Why?'

'I wondered how she seemed to you,' the doctor said. 'Did she seem her normal self?'

'I don't really know her well enough to say what her normal self is like,' Sara said. 'I thought actually she was rather upset because she thought that no one was taking any notice of its being her eightieth birthday.'

'Seriously upset? A bit more than normally upset?'

'Look here,' Oliver said sharply, 'are you dropping hints that that might have brought on a stroke? Or are you—are you suggesting that she might somehow have committed suicide? What's put that into your head?'

'The taste of the coffee in the jug,' the doctor said. 'There's a little left. You didn't try it yourself?'

'No,' Oliver said.

'I took a sip of it,' Stamforth said. 'Can't tell you exactly why I did. Automatic, almost. And it's distinctly peculiar. Very bitter.'

'She liked her coffee very strong and bitter,' Oliver said. 'She always got it from London. Continental roast, quite black. And she always made it herself, because she said Mrs Worth never got it right.'

'Yes, I see.' The doctor sounded doubtful. 'In any case, I don't think it ought to be touched. Don't wash it up. And perhaps . . .' An uneasy frown creased his forehead.

'Well?' Oliver said impatiently.

'That's all, just for the moment. Don't wash anything up. Later, perhaps . . .'

'What were you going to say?' Oliver asked.

'You see, if it does look like suicide, we'll have to call the police in. But for the moment, until we've got her to hospital—' He was interrupted by a ring at the door. 'That'll be the ambulance. We've been lucky. They aren't always so quick.'

He went out to meet the ambulance men and to direct proceedings.

Meg, coming downstairs, said that she would go to the hospital with her aunt in the ambulance. For a moment it looked as if Oliver intended to argue that it was he who ought to go, but then made up his mind that it might be best if a woman went with her. She put her hands on his shoulders and gave him a quick kiss and murmured, 'She'll be all right, don't worry so. Anyway, I'll telephone as soon as they can tell me anything.'

She followed the stretcher that the ambulance men were carrying out to the street. Oliver followed her, then as they heard the sound of the ambulance driving away, he came back into the drawing-room.

'I don't believe you for a moment,' he said to Stamforth. 'You aren't serious about it, are you?'

'That it could be suicide?' the doctor said. 'I know it's unlikely, but it's a possibility one's got to consider. That coffee . . .' He shook his head.

'If you like, to show you what I think, I'll go and drink the rest of it myself,' Oliver offered.

As if the doctor feared that he might really do this, he caught him by the arm.

'I said, don't touch it. Don't touch anything in the room. Has the door got a key?'

'I think so. I'm not sure. I think all our rooms have keys, though we never use them.'

'If it has one, we'll lock the door and give the key to General Schofield to look after. All right with you, General?'

'Yes, yes, of course, if I can be of help in any way,' the General answered. 'But I don't believe for a moment in your idea of suicide. I'm sure it's a stroke. Althea wasn't in the least a suicidal type. Much too strong-minded. We all know she's been very worried because she believed Oliver and Celia were going to get married and were going to leave her, but she'd never kill herself on account of that.'

'No, we know what she intended to do about that,' Celia Hancock said with acid in her voice. 'She wanted us all to know. She was changing her will and leaving all she had to Meg, instead of to Oliver. I believe her solicitor was coming to see her tomorrow to get her instructions. When you're arranging a thing like that, you don't commit suicide.'

'I'm not sure that you don't,' Ron said. He had sat down on a sofa and the children had sat down on either side of him. He put an arm round each. 'You think you've made up your mind to do something pretty vicious, and then you find you don't really want to. And you think instead of how to do something that's going to make everyone very sorry for the way they've treated you.'

'But where could she have got the stuff, whatever it was?' Oliver asked. He turned back to the doctor. 'That bitter taste you're talking about, what could it be?'

'Can't say,' Dr Stamforth answered. 'Might be a barbiturate possibly.'

'But where could she have got that?' Oliver repeated. 'You people don't prescribe it any more, do you?'

'Only for epilepsy,' Stamforth answered.

'And she wasn't an epileptic,' Oliver said.

'But she'd got a friend who is,' the General said. 'Poor Miss Hardingford, with whom Althea used to play bridge. Yes, I'm almost sure I remember her telling me that she was epileptic.'

'And you're suggesting she stole some of Miss Hardingford's pills?' Oliver said contemptuously. 'When is she supposed to have done that?'

'No, no, of course I don't mean that,' General Schofield said. 'But now I think perhaps I'd better do what Stamforth suggested and get the key of Althea's room. If after all Althea should die and there was any question about signing the death certificate . . . Oliver, my dear boy, I'm so sorry, I shouldn't have said that. All the same, Stamforth's in a position of great responsibility and I think we should do what he wants.'

'Thanks, General,' Stamforth said. 'I'll go and get the key for you.'

He went quickly out of the room.

As if absent-mindedly, the General popped a triangle of smoked salmon into his mouth. Then he said, 'Children, why don't you come and eat these things up? It would be a pity to waste them.'

The children at first seemed to be of two minds about the propriety of accepting his suggestion at such a time, but then they got up and tentatively approached the table and helped themselves. Then they each ate something more from a plate on the table, and then something more, and soon they were making a very good supper out of what was there, though in silence and standing close together, as if to give each other support in doing something which was perhaps not altogether good-mannered, even if they had been urged to do it by the General.

Dr Stamforth had appeared after having been only a minute or two out of the room and gave a key to the General.

'You'll hear something from the hospital soon,' he said. 'I can't stay any longer myself. I ought to have been at the surgery some time ago. But I'll let you know if I hear anything.'

Oliver saw him to the door and, coming back into the room after he had gone, slumped down in a chair, leant his elbows on his knees and covered his face in his hands. His whole body was shaking slightly.

Paul Fryer turned towards him.

'Oliver, wouldn't you sooner that those of us who aren't family went home?' he said. 'There's not much we can do to help.'

The General answered quickly, before Oliver had had time to lift his face from his hands. 'I think we should all wait here till we've had a call from the hospital. Meg will phone us as soon as she can.'

'In that case, I think we'd better have a drink all round,' Ron said. 'Not the champagne. Lucky we hadn't got around to opening it. But I could do with a stiff whisky. So could Oliver. No, old chap,' he added as Oliver seemed about to get up as if he felt that it was his duty as host to provide drinks for his guests, 'I'll see to it.'

He went out of the room, returning with a tray with glasses, a bottle of whisky and a jug of water.

'Same thing for everybody?' he asked, looking round. 'Sara?'

'Please,' she said.

He poured the drink and held it out to her.

'Celia?' he said. 'Kay?'

Celia nodded and Kay said, 'Yes, please, Ron. Oh, isn't all this awful? Oliver, I'm so sorry.'

Something extraordinary happened to Sara as she heard it, and suddenly she felt a shock that was almost one of fear, though why it should frighten her she could not have said. The fact was, however, that the voice that she had just heard sounded eerily familiar. Until then she had not heard Kay speak above a whisper, but the fact was that her normal voice sounded just like the voice that Sara had heard having an absurd conversation with no one on her answerphone.

Or was she mistaken? Probably she was. She began to have second thoughts about it. Only a little while ago she had thought she had recognized Jill's voice, and that it should have been the child's, amusing herself by leaving a meaningless message on the tape, seemed much more probable than that it should be that of this young woman. All the same, Sara began to wonder about Kay Eldridge. What was she doing here? She seemed to have no particular connection with anyone in the family. Celia Hancock was Oliver's fiancée. Meg and Ron were his cousins. The twins were their children. General Schofield was an old friend of Mrs Cannon's. Paul Fryer was the tenant from the base-ment, as Sara was the tenant from the top-floor flat. But what was Kay Eldridge's relation to the family?

She was having a low-voiced conversation now with Paul, and Sara began to wonder if that was the connection. Yet even if it were, that would not explain what was on the answerphone. Really the most probable explanation of it, Sara thought, was the one that she had thought of earlier, that it had been the child Jill, deliberately parodying some-one's voice, perhaps actually Kay's, which was high and fluting.

The child must have been doing it to entertain some audience, perhaps only Nick, pretending that she was re-ceiving replies, and the fact that what she said was being recorded had really meant nothing to her. She might have rung the number of the top-floor flat believing it still to be empty. The Kimberleys had perhaps not heard yet that it had been re-let, and when she had heard Sara's voice, giving her name and asking her to leave a message, she had simply not wanted to give up her game.

The telephone rang.

It was within Oliver's reach and he grabbed it and said, 'Yes? ... Yes? ... Oh ... You're sure? There's no question ...? Yes.'

He put the phone down slowly and gently as if that might somehow soften what he had to say. Celia went to him quickly and put an arm round his shoulders.

'She's gone?' she said.

'Dead on arrival,' he answered, then gave a shudder that shook his whole body and started weeping violently.

Celia sat down beside him and drew his head down on to her breast. He did not hold her but lay in her grasp like a child. It struck Sara just then that if he had lost one mother, he had managed to acquire another.

'Then I think there's something we've got to do,' General Schofield said. 'And the sooner we get it over, the better. I'll call Inspector Dalling. He's a good friend of mine. He'll be tactful and kind.'

He reached for the telephone that Oliver had just put down and started dialling.

CHAPTER 4

Kind and tactful Detective-Inspector Dalling who arrived shortly afterwards was accompanied by Detective-Constable Miller who seemed prepared to be every bit as kind and tactful as his superior. That is to say, he seemed to assume that the proper thing for him to do was to say nothing and not to appear too obviously to want to know just why he had been brought there.

Dalling was a thickset man in his forties, with dark brown

hair, brown eyes under craggy eyebrows, a short nose, a tight-lipped mouth and a round chin which would probably show folds under it before he was much older. He appeared to be on friendly terms with General Schofield and yet to distance himself from whatever had happened in the room into which he had been brought. As friend or as enemy he would probably maintain that impersonal air of distance. Miller was about thirty, tall, bony and fair-haired. After a short talk with the General and one with Oliver Cannon, Dalling did not appear to feel that there was any need to keep everyone in the room. He was willing that Sara and Paul should each go to their flats and told Celia Hancock and Kay Eldridge that they could return to their homes if they would leave him their addresses. Celia, however, standing close to Oliver, said that she would prefer to remain. The Inspector seemed to be in two minds about the Kimberleys. He obviously did not want to keep the children there; on the other hand they were a part of the family. It ended with his suggesting that Meg should take the children home, while Ron should remain. He took for granted that the General would remain.

Sara was glad to escape to her flat upstairs, while Paul went down to his, accompanied, she thought, by Kay. As she entered her sitting-room she saw the red light on her answerphone and found that while she had been out she had had two calls from friends in London. Each had left a message, asking her to call them back when she got in, but neither, she thought, would be about anything urgent and though she could have called them back immediately, she put it off, feeling that the last thing that she wanted to do just then was to have a cheerful chat with even the best of friends.

She wished that she had some whisky in the flat, but all she had was sherry and after the whisky that she had just been drinking downstairs she thought it would feel somewhat flat. All the same, after roaming restlessly about the flat for a little while, she poured out a glass of sherry and sat down with it in a chair by the small open window. She supposed that presently she would begin to think of getting herself something for supper, but like the telephone calls from her friends, she felt that was something that could wait.

It was about nine o'clock when her doorbell rang and she found Detective-Inspector Dalling and Detective-Constable Miller on the landing.

'I'm sorry to disturb you,' Dalling said, 'but there are one or two things we'd like to ask you, if you don't mind. Probably unimportant, but there's always a chance they may be helpful.'

'Then after all you don't think it was a stroke that killed Mrs Cannon,' Sara said. 'Does it really look like suicide?'

She let them into the room and closed the door behind them.

'Could be, could be,' Dalling replied. He looked round. 'You live here alone, do you?'

'Yes,' Sara said.

'Been here long?' he asked.

'Three days.'

'Ah,' he remarked, 'I didn't think the place had what you might call a lived-in look. Your own furniture?'

'No, I've taken the place furnished by the week from Mrs Cannon. I'm doing a job of work in Edgewater. I don't suppose I'll be here long.'

'Ah,' he said again. 'And what sort of work would that be?'

'Sit down, won't you?' She sat down herself in the chair by the window, leaving the men to find chairs for themselves. 'I'm working with General Schofield on his memoirs. But what has that to do with this tragic affair of Mrs Cannon's?'

'Working with him on his memoirs, are you?' Dalling said, ignoring her question. 'That means you're what's called a ghost, doesn't it?'

The word irritated Sara. It seemed derogatory. However, she said, 'Very well, I'm a ghost. And I'll try to walk away through the wall if you want me to show you my powers.'

'I'm sorry, have I said the wrong thing?' Dalling said, while Miller, Sara thought, gave a chuckle which he tried to conceal by passing a hand over his mouth. 'I don't know much about you literary people, or how you describe your-selves. I've sometimes thought I'd write my own memoirs when I retire. I've had a very interesting life. But I'm sure I'd need someone like you to help me with it. Meanwhile, we've just been talking to Mr Fryer and it seems that although he's got a perfectly good job at that exclusive school, Granborough, he fancies he can write thrillers. And instead of letting us ask him the questions we wanted to ask, he spent the time asking us very searching questions about police procedure. Made things difficult for us, really.'

'But what are the questions you want to ask?' Sara demanded. 'I don't think you came up here to ask if I was a ghost.'

'Well, there's something a literary lady like you might be able to tell us,' he answered. 'No, I don't mean tell us. But it's something on which you might have an opinion. I've been gathering opinions from everyone on the same matter. It's just this. Suppose you were thinking of killing yourself, suppose you'd just drunk a cup of coffee laced with a lot of some drug, say a barbiturate, would you lie down and calmly read a book, even a Graham Greene, until the stuff knocked you out? Do you think you could really do that?'

Sara began to think she understood the drift of his ques-tioning.

'Was that what she was doing before her collapse?' she asked.

'It isn't by any means certain,' he said. 'But a book was on the floor beside the bed and looked as if she'd dropped it there when she had her stroke, or fell asleep, or whatever. And even that, of course, isn't certain. The book might have been there since, say, the evening before, if she had a habit of reading for a time when she went to bed at night.'

'You could check that easily enough by questioning Mrs Worth,' Sara said. 'But I think she'd probably have made the bed and tidied the room when she arrived in the morning. I don't think she'd have left a book lying on the floor.'

Dalling nodded. 'Yes, we'll get around to that. She doesn't answer her telephone. Her husband says it's her bingo evening. So for the moment we haven't been able to speak to her, though someone will be going round to see her sometime soon. But you haven't answered my question, Mrs Marriott. If you'd just taken enough poison to kill yourself and were waiting for it to take effect, would you be able to lie quietly, reading a good book?'

'I'm sure I shouldn't,' Sara said.

'What do you think you'd do?'

'I'm afraid that's something I've never thought about.'

Yet this was not altogether true. There had been a time, not so very long ago, when the thought of killing herself had been alarmingly attractive to Sara. The aching pain of living, with its emptiness and futility, had been something from which it would have been a consoling thing to escape. Or so she had sometimes tried to convince herself, knowing all the time that the feeling did not go deep. She knew that even when she had been in the worst throes of depression she had still strongly clung to life. To be unloved, unneeded, left to fight the demon of a kind of self-contempt alone, was not the worst thing that could happen to her. All the same, if she had been able to think of some really easy and painless way of putting an end to her existence, there would have been something very tempting about it.

'What's making you think of suicide?' she asked. 'Was Dr Stamforth right that there was something queer about the coffee?'

'We'll know more about that tomorrow,' Dalling replied. 'It's of course being checked.'

'You say you've been asking everyone that question about whether they could lie reading after they'd swallowed some poison,' Sara said. 'What did they say?'

'Without exception what you've said yourself. But they had different ideas about how they'd spend the time while they were waiting for something to happen. Mr Cannon said he'd listen to Beethoven's Ninth Symphony. Very superior. Miss Hancock said she'd try writing a letter to her oldest friend, telling her why she was doing what she was, and if she was still alive when she'd finished it she'd just lie down and wait. Mr Kimberley said he'd get a bottle of whisky and drink the lot. General Schofield said nothing would ever make him consider taking his own life. Mr Fryer, I'm sorry to say, didn't seem to take the question very seriously, because all he said he'd do was destroy the last chapter of the book he'd just finished, so that no one would ever know whodunnit, and they could have competitions to see who could come up with the best solution.'

'And Miss Eldridge?' Sara asked.

'She'd gone home before we got around to asking her.'

So she had not stayed long in Paul Fryer's flat.

'Do you know something, Inspector,' Sara said, 'I'm not sure that your question deserves to be taken any more seriously than Mr Fryer took it. I don't know what it is you really want to know, but I've a feeling you haven't really got around yet to asking it.'

He shook his head. 'You're quite wrong, Mrs Marriott. When you get a feeling yourself, just a feeling, that something isn't quite what it appears, it can be very helpful to know how the thing's affected other people. Now may I ask you a quite different question? I believe you saw Mrs Cannon just before lunch today.'

Sara nodded.

'And what opinion did you form of her mental condition?'

'That's what Dr Stamforth asked me,' Sara said.

'Well, would you mind telling me what you thought of it?'

'I don't suppose I thought very much about it at all. We just had a drink and chatted for a little while. She was upset because she thought that no one was taking any notice of its being her eightieth birthday. Several people seem to have sent her presents, but it was a party she wanted. And that her family were laying on a little surprise party for her had been kept such a secret from her that she was feeling really hurt. And then she said something about making a new will and leaving everything to her niece, Mrs Kimberley. She was very bitter about her son's probably marrying and leaving Edgewater to go to a job in Canada.'

'She said that?' He looked grave. 'She quite definitely said it? It wasn't just that she was rambling a bit because she was upset?'

'I thought she meant it,' Sara answered. 'And she seemed to have told all her family about it, because even the Kimberley children knew about it.'

'I see. Well, thank you, Mrs Marriott. That's been very valuable.'

He and the Detective-Constable took their leave.

Sara thought of making a ham sandwich for herself, but put off actually doing so, still sitting by the window and gazing out in an unseeing way. The Downs were visible from the window, a smooth green curve against a sky that was darkened by the coming evening, and she could see the chestnuts that lined the road that led towards them, though first to the Heath, with its lazy stream where at this hour people were probably walking their dogs for their evening outing.

It troubled her that she did not know what to feel about the events of the evening. Death was of course a shock and deeply impressive, but in this case it was simply because it had happened, so to speak, on her own doorstep and it really meant no more to her than those she might have read of in a newspaper, deaths on the road, for instance, or in some house that had gone on fire miles away, killing all the people in it. She had hardly known and had not much liked what she had seen of Mrs Cannon. She had seemed an aggressive, selfish woman. But the two men coming and questioning her had left Sara nervous and restless. Instead of the ham sandwich, her thoughts turned towards another drink. She was thinking of getting up to pour it out when her doorbell rang.

This time it was Paul Fryer who mounted the stairs and arrived on the landing. She felt extraordinarily pleased to see him. She would have felt pleased to see anyone just then except those two detectives, who for a moment, as she went to the door, she had thought might be returning.

'Come in,' she said.

'I was thinking we might go out,' Paul said, though he came forward into the room. 'Have you had any supper yet?'

'No,' she replied.

'Neither have I. I can't seem to settle down to getting anything, and I thought there was a chance you might be in the same state and that perhaps we might go out and eat something together at Pietro's. Does it strike you as a good idea?'

Pietro's was one of the very few restaurants in Edgewater, not as expensive as the Red Lion, but with tolerable food.

'A very good one,' Sara said. 'I didn't seem to want

anything here, but I'd never have made up my mind to go out alone. Do you know how all the others are?'

'I only know Ron's gone home with the children and Celia is staying with Oliver and Kay's gone home, she lives in a little bungalow on the other side of the Heath, very convenient for her job, as she works in the Agricultural College.'

'So that big building on the other side of the Heath is the Agricultural College, is it?' Sara said as they started down the stairs. 'What does Kay do there?'

'She's Oliver's secretary. Nice girl. She's going to miss him if he really leaves.'

'But it won't affect her job, will it?'

'Oh no, she'll be handed on to his successor.'

'And is he really going to leave, do you think?'

They had reached the street and started along it towards the little turning out of it where Pietro had his small restaurant. The street lamps had just come on but there were very few people about. Though the sun had gone, the sky to the west still had a sombre, russet glow.

'I shouldn't think he could answer that himself at the moment,' Paul said as they walked along side by side. 'I always thought one of his reasons for going was so that he could get away from his mother, or at least that one of the reasons why Celia was so keen on his going was to get him away from her. I don't know much about what it's like myself to have an overpoweringly possessive parent. I'm one of a family of five and I always felt I was lucky if I got any time at all from my father or mother.'

'It isn't a thing that's troubled me either,' Sara said. 'My father died when I was a child and my mother remarried and has lived for years in America, but I was left here at school at Granborough except just during the holidays, and she and my stepfather were perfectly ready to let me stay in England when I thought of going to a university.'

'And you got married over here, did you?'

'Yes.'

They had reached the turning to Pietro's. It had one window with a door beside it with a glass panel through which light shone out into the street. Inside, it was lit by strip-lights placed here and there among old beams in a low ceiling. There were only a dozen tables in a long, narrow room and only three of these were occupied, the usual hour for dinner there being a good deal earlier. Pietro himself, a small, portly Italian from the East End of London, with the little black hair he had left brushed across the crown of his shiny round head, an accent that had kept traces of Italian under the dominant cockney, and small, dark, anxious eyes, showed them to a table in the depths of the room and took their order.

They both chose the cold chicken consommé and mushroom omelettes, and after some discussion between Paul and Pietro, a bottle of the house wine. To Sara's surprise, she felt quite ready to eat.

'And we were saying . . .' Paul said while they waited for their order to be brought. 'But what were we saying? What were we talking about?'

'About possessive parents,' Sara said, though she remembered that they had just begun to talk about something else before they entered the restaurant. But she did not want to go back to that.

'And you said you'd been at Granborough yourself,' Paul said. 'What do you think about that now?'

'What do you think about it yourself, teaching there?' she asked. 'Is there anything very special about it?'

'Oh, I like it well enough,' he answered, 'but I don't suppose I shall stay for long. I don't think I was meant to be a teacher. If I find I can make a living by writing . . . But what did it mean to you as a child?'

'I think I was quite reasonably happy. And I had my

first experience of falling in love. It was on a rainy day during my first term when I was eleven years old and it was too wet for us to go out of doors for break in the morning, and we were fooling around in the gym, and suddenly a boy of about my own age, whom I don't think I'd ever exchanged a word with, rushed across the room and knocked me over backwards. And I promptly fell in love with him. And I remained faithful to him for four or five years.'

'So cave-man tactics still work, even in this day and age,' Paul said.

'It would seem so, even though I don't suppose he knew why he did what he did, any more than I knew why I responded to it with such emotion.'

'And did he stay faithful to you?'

'Good lord, no. He'd had his passionate impulse and after that had no more interest in me.'

'Did that hurt?'

'Horribly.' She laughed. 'It really did, you know. And I think his image was somehow imprinted on my imagination so that I remained awfully likely to fall in love with anyone of roughly the same type.'

'And what was he like?'

'Oh, slim, well-built, fair-haired, blue-eyed, and very good-natured, but not too clever.'

'He wasn't clever?'

'Not in the least.'

'And does that mean you've remained frightened of brains as good as your own ever since?'

Their chicken consommé arrived at that point. It was jellified and probably out of a tin, but seemed pleasantly cool in the warm, airless room, where one or two fans kept the hot air stirring but seemed to do little to reduce its heat. The house wine was just drinkable. For a moment Sara found herself reflecting that there was something reassuring about the fact that the man facing her across the small table was not slim and fair-haired and blue-eyed, but was solidly built and had dark curly hair and dark eyes behind thick glasses which looked extremely intelligent. This utter contrast with her old memory made her feel unusually comfortable with him. In fact, for once, she found that she actually wanted to talk.

'It might have been better for me if it had,' she said. 'My husband had the physical attributes of my early love, though not much else in common with him.'

'His good nature, for instance.' Paul seemed really interested. 'Didn't that go deep enough?'

'Oh no, his good nature was absolutely genuine,' Sara said. 'He was extremely good to me. But he was good to a lot of other people too and I then made the discovery that when it came to a husband I was very possessive. And he had such very good reasons to prove to me that this was quite wrong of me, and that our life would be ever so much richer if I'd get over it. And I've always believed that he was right and that I was to blame for the misery I went through when our marriage fell apart.' She paused. 'Only I don't know why I'm talking like this.'

'My guess is it's something you've been needing to do for a long time,' Paul said, 'and that what happened this evening, I mean our being brushed by death, even though it was that of a comparative stranger, has stirred up all kinds of buried things in both of us. I've been thinking of the first girl I was ever in love with. When she got married if was a kind of death for me. I immediately went off and had an affair with a girl who didn't mean anything to me and it was engrossing and violent and taught me a great deal about myself, but when she got married too I sent her the most expensive present I could afford and shed tears, but they were actually all for that first love of mine, who by then had three children and a splendid job with the

BBC and a second husband. But what went wrong with Marriott? Were you inordinately jealous?'

She nodded. 'You see, he was so dreadfully open about everything. He told me every detail about what he was doing and said that that only showed how much he loved and trusted me. And his first love-affair after we were married happened to be with my best friend, and the funny thing is she's still my best friend, we don't seem able to turn against one another. But I hate her too at times, of course, only I don't seem able to find anyone else I like as much.'

'Was she at Granborough too?' he asked.

'Yes, we met there on our very first day.'

'And your husband, was he there too?'

'No, I met him at University College, years later.'

'And of course he met your friend through you and you were so delighted that they liked one another.'

'But he didn't start his affair with her until after we'd got married. I don't think he'd known much about sex himself till then.'

'But then he told you all about it.'

'Yes, everything.'

'Honesty can be horribly cruel, can't it? How long did it take you to make up your mind you couldn't stand it?'

'About a couple of years, I suppose. His idea was that I should go and do likewise and then we could confide in one another and love each other more than ever. And I had a try at it, but somehow it didn't take. So we just started seeing less and less of one another, but it took us quite a while to make up our minds to a divorce. And then it came along very slowly, because apparently we'd made every mistake, legally speaking, that we could have, so it was complicated. If only we hadn't gone in for all that honesty, it would have been over much sooner.'

'And your friend who started the trouble, what's happened to her?'

'Oh, she left him long ago. She trained as a nurse and got a job doing relief work in one of those African countries where they're always having famines and droughts and civil wars. I forget which one it is at the moment.'

'But you still see her sometimes?'

'She comes home on leave occasionally. I nearly went back with her the last time she came over, but the divorce was on the move by then and it seemed sensible to see it through.'

'And then you came to Edgewater to write General Schofield's memoirs for him. But what will you do when that's finished?'

'Hope someone else wants me to ghost his memoirs for him, I suppose. There—I've admitted that that's what I am, a ghost. I usually try to find other words for it. I don't like the idea of being just a shadow in someone else's life. But I've still to discover what I really want to do. I'm a very negative sort of person, I'm afraid.'

'Some bright psychologist might say it was all because that idiot boy knocked you over backwards when you were eleven years old.'

'And he might even be right.'

'I wonder what happened to him.'

'I haven't any idea.'

'And you aren't curious about him?'

'Not in the least.'

'I'm glad to hear it. Of course, teaching at Granborough, one sees that sort of thing happening all the time, and surprisingly often it ends in marriage, which I sometimes feel is almost incestuous, though I dare say it's quite likely to be happy. But our prejudice against incest is still very strong, isn't it, compared with all the others we've shed? I've sometimes thought what a temptation it must be for twins. I can't help wishing the Kimberley twins weren't quite as united as they are, though with luck they'll grow out of it. But their father does everything he can to keep them together, under his own wing. We were talking about possessive parents, weren't we? That's a fairly acute case of it. Some people think it's so charming that he should care for them so much. They think it's a very attractive characteristic of his. But I'd be happier if he weren't around the school so much.'

'What does their mother think about it?'

'Meg? It's very difficult to discover what Meg thinks about anything except the importance of her sculpture.'

'And is it any good?'

'I'm no judge. I rather like what I've seen of it and I think she may be beginning to make a name for herself. But she's not demonstrative like Ron, though for all I know she's as devoted to the twins as he is.'

'This fact that they won't be inheriting Mrs Cannon's money after all she said about it, is that going to mean a lot to them?'

'I'm sure suddenly discovering you aren't going to be nearly as rich as you thought you were for even a little while would mean a good deal to almost everybody.'

'Yes, but do they really need the money? Are they hard up?'

'I don't think so. They could hardly keep two children at Granborough if they were. But I don't think you could call them rich. I believe the farm's a fairly successful one, though nothing spectacular.'

'Paul, do you believe Mrs Cannon committed suicide?'

Their consommé had been replaced by their omelettes and Pietro had just been to their table, topping up their wine-glasses. But even when he had left them, Paul did not reply at once. He did not meet Sara's gaze, but looked away down the room, frowning a little.

She added, 'That man Dalling doesn't, does he?'

Returning her look, it was as if he had not heard her question.

'I suppose I shall have to move from my flat,' he said. 'A pity. I like it. But Oliver's almost certain to want to sell the house now, and a sitting tenant doesn't add to the value of a property.'

She felt vexed that he had so deliberately ignored what she had asked him. However, she said, 'Hasn't a sitting tenant some rights? Is the furniture your own? I thought you couldn't be turned out if you'd taken the place unfurnished.'

'You may be right,' he said, 'but I shouldn't like to get into a row with Oliver. We've been quite good friends and I haven't such a passionate sense of possession of the place that I think it would be worth the trouble to have a fight about it. It'll be a nuisance, having to look for somewhere else, but I don't suppose there'll be any desperate hurry.'

'You're sure he will sell the house, are you?'

'If he takes that job in Toronto, yes, for certain. Why should he keep it?'

'But suppose he changes his mind and doesn't go. You said yourself you thought one of his reasons for going was to get away from his mother. If he and Celia stay here, wouldn't that apartment he's in now suit them quite well?'

'I've no idea what Celia thinks about it. For that matter, I don't know what Oliver really does. He lived there because his mother wouldn't move out of it. And he'll be a rich man now and able to pick and choose.'

'Yes, obviously it's fortunate for him she died today and not tomorrow. If she'd had time to make her new will he'd have lost quite heavily, I suppose. But Paul . . .'

'Yes?' he said when she paused, though she was fairly sure that he knew what was coming.

'You haven't answered my question, do you believe Mrs Cannon committed suicide?'

'As you said, Dalling doesn't,' he said. 'All because of a book on the floor.'

'But suppose Dr Stamforth's right and they find barbiturate or something in the coffee?'

He gave her a long, thoughtful look. Behind his thick glasses, his dark eyes were very unrevealing.

'You're trying to get me to say I think it might have been murder,' he said.

She answered quickly, 'I'm not trying to get you to say anything.'

'I think you are. I think you've got murder at the back of your mind.'

'Well, haven't you? Isn't that why you've got around so quickly to working out what may be going on in mine?'

He gave a short laugh. 'I admit it's on my mind, but that's mostly because I've spent most of today at work on my book describing the particularly foul and brutal murder of a villainous old judge who deserved to be murdered anyway, and I've managed to get seven possible suspects lined up, all in the same chapter.'

'While here at the moment we've only one, who of course is Oliver, and I'm sure Mrs Cannon didn't deserve to be murdered. But I do find that book on the floor worrying. But perhaps it'll turn out that there wasn't any barbiturate in the coffee and it was a stroke that killed her.'

'Do you feel like some coffee now?'

'Actually, I don't think I do.'

'I'm sure Pietro won't lace it with barbiturate.'

'I was just thinking that if I drink coffee so late, it's rather likely to keep me awake.'

But it was not coffee that prevented Sara sleeping that night.

It was in its way a small thing, and perhaps it would not

have affected her as it did if the events of the day had not left her in a more tensely nervous state than usual. It was something that happened after she had said good night to Paul and climbed the stairs to her flat. First, she found that the door of it was unlocked. That by itself would not have troubled her, for she could not remember having locked it when she went out. Her flat in Windsor had a Yale lock so she had only to pull the door shut behind her for it to lock automatically. But the door here had a mortice lock, so she had to remember to turn the key and take it with her when she went out, which she often forgot to do. Anyway, it hardly felt worth bothering about here in quiet Edgewater, and with a flat that had nothing of value in it.

But once she had entered the flat and locked the door on the inside, which she did trouble to do at night, she thought that she would look to see if there had been any messages left for her on her answerphone. Its red light was not on, which should have told her that there would be nothing. All the same, she thought that she would check it.

Then something very disturbing happened, something that kept her awake for most of the night, trying to guess what had occurred here while she had been out. It was simply that the tape on which had been recorded the odd, one-sided conversation that had worried her earlier in the day had vanished. It actually looked as if someone had come in and stolen it.

CHAPTER 5

Next morning Sara arrived as usual at ten o'clock at General Schofield's house in the High Street. He let her in, but when she was settled in the red leather chair by the fireplace and had arranged her tape-recorder and her notebook and was ready to start work, he did not sit down in the chair facing her, but remained standing behind it and gave an embarrassed cough.

'Do you know, I really don't feel like working today?' he said. 'After what happened to poor Althea yesterday I don't seem able to think just about myself. I know it's wasting your time, but I hope you'll forgive me. Would you care for a cup of coffee?'

'That would be very nice,' Sara said, 'and I know how you must feel, so please don't apologize.'

'She was such a very old friend, you see,' he said. 'I suppose I knew her better than anyone. Perhaps better in a way than Oliver did. Children often don't understand their parents, even when they've grown up and you'd think they ought to be able to do so. But so much happened in their parents' lives before they even came into existence, sometimes the most important things. Now I'll just see about that coffee.'

He left the room for a minute or two to request the little elderly man who came in on certain mornings of the week to clean the house for him to make the coffee. Sara knew that he did his own cooking, though on the occasions when he felt like entertaining his friends, he usually took them to the Red Lion.

Returning to the room, he sat down and said, 'If you'll forgive my saying so, I think you're looking rather tired yourself. Perhaps we've all been pretty badly affected by the tragedy yesterday.'

'It's true I didn't sleep much,' Sara said. 'A peculiar thing had happened and I couldn't stop thinking about it. I dare say it wasn't really anything very important, but the trouble is I can't make sense of it.'

'Something connected with Althea's death?' he asked.

'I don't really see how it could be,' she answered. 'But it worries me all the same.'

'Try telling me about it,' he suggested, 'or is it something you'd sooner keep to yourself?'

'No, I'd like to tell you about it. It's just that it'll be a bit difficult to explain, because the evidence has gone missing . . . You see, there's an answerphone in the flat, which I suppose the people who lived there before me left behind and I'd left it switched on yesterday morning when I came here, though I wasn't really expecting a call, but when I got back—that was after I'd had my drink with Mrs Cannon— I saw the red light on and knew there was a message for me. But it was such a strange message . . .'

She paused as the coffee was brought into the room.

'A strange message?' the General said when they were alone again.

'Yes, I can't remember the actual words, but it was a woman's voice and it began, "Darling, it's me . . ." Then there was a little pause, then it went on, just as if someone had answered, asking if it was really all right about the party. Then there was another pause, then some more about not being sure if Mrs Cannon liked her, but promising she'd be there at six o'clock, and ending up saying, "Lots of love". None of it sounded important, but what was so odd, you see, was that it sounded just like one side of a conversation. Only you can't hold conversations with answerphones, so how was she getting her replies?'

He frowned thoughtfully. 'I agree with you that it's strange. But what did you mean when you said that the evidence had gone missing?'

'Well, yesterday evening I went out to dinner with Paul Fryer,' Sara said. 'Neither of us felt like getting a meal for ourselves, so we went to Pietro's. And when I got back to the flat afterwards I found that the tape had vanished. I'm afraid someone got into the flat while I was away and stole it.'

'That's certainly very strange. It sounds as if it may have

been more important to someone than you thought it was. Had you left your flat locked?'

'No, I'm afraid I hadn't. I'm rather careless about things like that.'

'And it was a woman's voice on the tape, you say?'

'So I thought when I heard it. But then I had an idea . . . I thought it was just possibly a child's voice, a child who was having a game, pretending to have a sophisticated sort of conversation on the telephone with someone who of course wasn't there. And then when I heard Jill at the party yesterday evening, pretending to be so grown-up about all the things she was eating, I suddenly wondered if it could have been her. But she was in London yesterday, wasn't she, so she couldn't have made the call, unless perhaps she made it earlier in the morning, before they set off? That's just possible, I suppose. But why come into my flat in the evening and steal the tape? There was nothing damaging on it.'

'Of course, Jill's a wonderful little actress,' he said, 'and has rather too much imagination for her own good. You should have seen her in the school play last Christmas, when she was the First Fairy in A *Midsummer Night's Dream*. Spoke her words beautifully. It was delightful. And if she made that call, I suppose she'd have done it when she had some sort of audience, in fact that would be why she did it, even if it was only Nick. She'd probably have known the number of the flat and thought it would be empty, as she'd have known the other tenants had left and might not have heard you'd moved in. And hearing your name on the answerphone may have puzzled her a bit, but not really worried her much.'

'Only why was the tape stolen last night?'

'Yes, as you say, why was it stolen?' He was stirring his coffee meditatively. 'Have you told anyone else about this?'

'No, it seemed too absurd to bother about. But I did have

a certain idea . . . Only that's absurd too, though perhaps now that the tape's been stolen one might think of it again. I wonder . . .' She paused, trying to make up her mind whether to go on. That very absurd idea she had had about the message—should she tell him about it?

The General waited for a moment, then said, 'Try it out on me. In my time I've listened to what sounded like the most extraordinary amount of utter absurdity in the way of suspicions, denunciations, and so on, and from time to time they've actually turned out to be absolutely correct.'

'Well, it's just that I wondered if the message could be some sort of code,' Sara said, feeling very self-conscious at the mere making of such a bizarre suggestion. 'That might explain the theft, mightn't it?'

He appeared to take her quite seriously.

'Now that's really a very interesting idea,' he said. 'And the fact that it was about a party when there was going to be a party in the evening was just a coincidence. Or could they be in any way connected? I can't think why any of Althea's guests should have had to leave anyone a message in code, but you did say Mrs Cannon's name was mentioned, didn't you, so of course there would have to be some sort of connection.'

'I told you it was an absurd idea,' Sara said unhappily, 'but I can't think of any explanation of the whole thing that isn't absurd.'

'Now wait a moment,' he said. 'Let's think this over carefully. Let's suppose that someone had a secret message of some sort to give to the couple who were living in the flat until a few days ago. That would mean that that couple weren't quite what they seemed. And what they seemed to be was a very ordinary, rather uninteresting, hard-working couple who lived very quietly and never gave Althea any trouble. But it might be important for them to seem to be like that, as a cover for something that was quite different.

And that something, whatever it was, would almost certainly have had to be criminal, wouldn't it, something to do with drugs, or spying, or receiving stolen property or whatnot? Such crimes do occur, I imagine, even in Edgewater. But when whoever was speaking heard your name, she must have realized that something was wrong, yet she went on talking. That's puzzling, isn't it, unless the couple who were to get the message sometimes changed their names, as a way of getting some sort of message to the speaker. And she only found out later in the day that they'd left and that it was really very important for her to get hold of the tape.' He drank some coffee. 'Oh dear, I think we're getting into very deep water.'

Instead of feeling, as she had a moment before, almost as if she might start crying, Sara burst out laughing.

'What wonderful melodramatic nonsense it is when you really examine it,' she said. 'Thank you for disposing of the idea.'

'Ah, but there's something I don't think we have disposed of,' the General said. 'The message itself. It's still as puzzling as ever and there's something about it I don't like at all, apart from the theft. I feel sure that whoever was talking, whether it was Jill or not, was doing it for an audience. There was someone there who could hear everything the speaker said and who thought she was holding a normal conversation. Now why should it be important to anyone to do that—?'

He broke off because at that moment the front doorbell rang.

He went to answer it and returned, bringing with him Detective-Inspector Dalling and Detective-Constable Miller.

Seeing Sara, Dalling said, 'Good morning, Mrs Marriott. This'll save us some trouble. We wanted a word with you this morning.'

'You've news about Mrs Cannon?' the General said.

Dalling nodded. The General offered them chairs, then returned to the one in which he had been sitting before their arrival.

'Yes, bad news, I'm afraid,' Dalling said. 'At least, I assume you'll think it's bad. We've been talking to Mr Cannon and we're going on to see Mr and Mrs Kimberley, but as you live so near the Cannons we thought we'd come here before going on to the farm. The fact is, Dr Stamforth's guess was quite correct. Mrs Cannon died of a heavy overdose of some barbiturate which she drank in the coffee that she'd made for herself after lunch.'

'So it was suicide after all,' General Schofield said. 'Poor woman, I'd never have believed it of her, even though I knew she could hardly bear the thought of parting with her son. I wonder if what really unbalanced her was her own idea of revenge. I mean, leaving all she had to her niece instead of to her son. Perhaps she suddenly saw that as a mean, ungenerous thing to do and couldn't forgive herself for having so nearly done it.'

Dalling did not look much impressed. 'Perhaps,' he said drily.

'But I imagine you haven't come here only to tell us this sad news,' General Schofield said. 'I should have heard about it in any case from Cannon. And he hasn't telephoned. I suppose he knew you were coming here and that there are probably some things you want to ask me. Is there any way in which I can help?'

'You may be able to explain one or two things that are rather puzzling,' Dalling replied. 'To begin with, barbiturates have a quite strong bitter taste which would have ruined normal coffee, and if she drank as much of it as it seems she did, that certainly suggests suicide. But Mrs Worth, the Cannons' daily help, has told us that Mrs

Cannon had virtually lost her sense of taste, as some old people do. Do you know anything about that?'

As if to himself the Constable murmured, '"Sans teeth, sans eyes, sans taste, sans everything . . ."' Then he looked startled at himself and, as his habit was, hid his mouth behind his hand. 'Sorry,' he said. 'It's just that I had to learn that by heart at school, and everything I learnt by heart when I was at school has stuck in my head ever since.'

It was the longest speech that Sara had heard him make.

'Didn't Mr Cannon tell you if Mrs Worth was right?' she asked.

'We saw her after we'd seen him,' Dalling answered, 'and he didn't mention it. But we thought General Schofield might know if it was true.'

'As a matter of fact, it was,' the General said. 'It started coming on two or three years ago. She complained about it a good deal, because she said she could no longer enjoy a good meal. She was very envious of me, because I was older than she was, yet my sense of taste is quite unimpaired. But she complained that she really got no pleasure any more from eating, for instance, the most excellent fresh salmon. But, Inspector—' He stopped and gave a suddenly startled stare at the detective.

'Yes, General?'

'Does it matter that she couldn't taste the drug in the coffee? I mean, if she'd put it there herself, it wouldn't have made much difference to her whether she could taste it or not.'

'*If* she put it there herself, yes, of course you're right,' Dalling said.

There was silence while the General digested this statement and Sara's mind went back to her discussion the evening before with Paul Fryer in Pietro's, and to a feeling that had lurked at the back of her mind ever since that

what had been said then was going to be said by someone
else sooner or later.

'But that means you think she may have been murdered!'
the General exploded.

'It's only that we've got to explore all the possibilities,'
Dalling said quietly, 'and I admit there's next to no evidence of murder. Just one or two things that don't quite fit
the picture of suicide. That book on the floor by her bed.
There may be some quite simple explanation of how it got
there, but what I can't believe is that she'd drink what she
knew was a lethal amount of her doctored coffee and then
quietly lie back to read until the drug overcame her and
the book fell out of her hand. And then there's the question
of how she got the drug. We don't know anything about
that.'

'Where would anyone get it nowadays,' the General
asked, 'other than from a doctor?'

'I believe someone with access to a laboratory might get
it,' Dalling answered. 'It's got its uses in some kinds of
scientific work, I believe.'

'So you're thinking of someone connected with the Agricultural College!' The General still sounded explosive.
'They'd have the stuff there, perhaps. So you're thinking of
Oliver Cannon. You're thinking he'd a motive, stopping his
mother changing her will. You're thinking he could come
and go in the house. But you don't know the man. He and
his mother may have got into a way of quarrelling recently,
but he was devoted to her. And if he was going to a good
job in Canada, he didn't desperately need the money. If
you're seriously thinking of murder and that Oliver Cannon
could have done it, you're wrong, absolutely wrong!'

'I don't believe I've said a word against Mr Cannon,'
Dalling said. 'Or against anybody. And the possibility of
murder is only something that has to be investigated, but
the fact is, as I said, the evidence of it is so slight that unless

we turn up something more than we've got, I should think it would be impossible to prove it.'

'Something more than you've got . . .' The General seemed to have calmed down as suddenly as he had blown up and to have become thoughtful. After a moment he looked at Sara. 'I don't see any possible connection, but I wonder, Mrs Marriott, if it would be a good idea for you to tell Inspector Dalling what you told me this morning. I mean about the message on your answerphone. It's a queer story and the theft last night is worrying, and perhaps he should be told about it, simply because it's so strange. What do you think yourself?'

'A theft?' Dalling said. 'Has something been stolen from you, Mrs Marriott?'

'Yes, but if I'm going to tell you about it, I'd better begin at the beginning,' Sara said, 'and it's a longish story.'

'Go ahead.'

She told him the story of the message on the answerphone and of the theft of the tape in the evening very much as she had told it to General Schofield. But she made no attempt to offer an explanation of what had happened. She said nothing about her guess that it might have been Jill playing a game, and not a word about her wild supposition that it could have contained a code. She told him only the facts of which she was certain.

'And I'm sorry I can't remember more exactly what was on the tape,' she said, 'but I didn't really listen to it very carefully. It seemed such nonsense.'

Dalling nodded. 'Yes, I understand that. Well, thank you for telling me about it. Possibly we'll be able to make some sense of it later. It's impossible to say at the moment if it's of any importance, but we're very interested just now in anything that doesn't fit normally into the ways of the household. Can you tell me at about what time you discovered what was on the tape?'

'I think it was about a quarter past one,' Sara said. 'I'd met Mrs Cannon when I got back to the house from my work here and I think that was at about half past twelve, and she asked me in for a drink and I stayed with her just a little while, then went upstairs and saw that there'd been a message for me.'

'So the message was left definitely before one o'clock, though we don't know how much earlier. At what time did you go out?'

'Just before ten o'clock.'

'So it was later than ten. Now do you mind telling me, Mrs Marriott, whether you stayed in your flat after you got back, or did you go out again?'

'Just a minute, just a minute!' the General interrupted. 'He's asking you for your alibi, Sara, and you don't have to tell him a thing if you don't want to.'

It was the first time he had called her Sara. She gave a slight smile.

'But I don't mind saying what I did,' she said. 'I went out to the Green Tree Café for lunch—I've been having my lunch there ever since I got here—then I went home again and did some work on General Schofield's book, then some time in the afternoon Mr Cannon came up and invited me to the party they were giving for his mother in the evening. I should think I was in the café from about half past one till two or a quarter past. Do you know when Mrs Cannon drank her coffee?'

'It was probably about two o'clock,' Dalling answered, 'but that's only a rough guess. The forensic people haven't come up with anything more exact yet, and perhaps won't be able to do so in any case, but Mrs Worth has told us that that was about Mrs Cannon's usual time for it.'

'So my alibi isn't absolutely watertight, is it?' Sara said.

'But mine is,' the General declaimed with some of his former excitement. 'From half past twelve until three o'clock I was at a luncheon at the Red Lion. It was the annual luncheon of the Edgewater Historical Society, of which I have been a member for at least fifteen years.'

'Thank you,' Dalling said. 'At the Red Lion, you say. That's just across the street from Mrs Cannon's house, isn't it, a couple of minutes' walk away? And I suppose there were a lot of people there and a good deal of coming and going. Just sometimes, you know, one can get lost in a crowd, if it's only for a few minutes. But of course that didn't happen to you, General, did it? Now we'll be going. And we'll think about that story of yours, Mrs Marriott. After all, it must mean something.'

That the Detective-Inspector, in casting a faint doubt on the soundness of the General's alibi, had only been teasing him, seemed fairly certain to Sara, but she was not at all sure how the General would take it. Would he, when he returned to the room after letting the two men out, be in a furious temper? Luckily he was not. It appeared, from the slightly self-conscious smile on his face, that he felt that if he had been made a fool of, it was his own fault.

'I'm an ass,' he remarked as he sat down again and finished the cold coffee that was left in his cup. 'I was quite wrong in the way I handled that man. I almost lost my temper with him and of course he paid me back for it. Now I've had an idea, Sara. I don't know what you'll think of it. You've a car, haven't you?'

'Yes,' she said.

'So have I, but I'm not very fond of driving any more. My eyes aren't what they were and I don't altogether trust the speed of my reactions. So except just around here in Edgewater, where I know every inch of the road, I hardly use it. The sensible thing would be to sell it, but I can't quite make up my mind to doing that. One's so used to having the thing, it would feel almost like cutting off a limb.

But I'd rather like to drive out to talk to the Kimberleys, and I was wondering if you'd take me. It's quite a pleasant drive.'

'Yes, of course I will,' Sara said. 'When do you want to go? Now?'

'No, that man Dalling said he was going out there after talking to us, didn't he? And I'd like a talk with Oliver first. So I was thinking about this afternoon, say about two o'clock. How would you feel about that?'

'Any time you like,' Sara answered.

'All right then, suppose you pick me up about two o'clock. And we can go along to the Cannon house straight away, because I suppose Oliver will have stayed at home. Poor fellow, this news must have been a fearful shock for him, even if that man hasn't been dropping hints to him about a possible murder, because if Althea really committed suicide, Oliver's going to be blaming himself for having been the cause. Come along, let's go.'

Together they walked down the High Street to the Cannons' house.

Sara went straight up to her flat, leaving the General to ring the Cannons' doorbell and to be admitted to their apartment, she supposed by Oliver. She would have lunch as usual at the Green Tree Café, she thought, and presently went there to eat some cold roast veal and salad and some apple pie. After it she returned to the flat and lay down for what she meant should be only a brief rest. Her almost sleepless night had left her very tired, but she had no intention of going to sleep. But simply because she did not in the least mean to do so and had no anxiety about it, she fell asleep almost immediately. It was about ten minutes to two when she awoke and realized that she must move very fast if she was to be punctual for her appointment.

In fact, she was only about five minutes late. The General was waiting for her, his face more solemn than she had ever seen it. He seemed somewhat absent-minded too and hardly spoke to her as he got into the car beside her and fastened his seat-belt, except to give her some directions.

'Straight ahead through the square, then bear right, then second on the left . . .' He paused. 'But of course you know this part of the world, don't you? Ron and Meg's farm is just beyond the village of Bolding. Do you remember the way to Bolding?'

Sara remembered it quite well. The village consisted of a single street with the school, Granborough, at one end of it and a pub called the Coach and Horses at the other. Most of the houses along the street were occupied by people in some way connected with the school, though the village also had a church, a village green with a duck-pond in the middle of it, and one shop. Driving along the street, according to the General's directions, Sara saw that the shop had very much increased in size and sophistication since she had been here last, having become almost a small supermarket, and the Coach and Horses advertised itself as a restaurant offering good country fare and had small tables and chairs under striped umbrellas set out in front of it. Otherwise not much was changed. The farm for which they were heading was about a mile further on, spread out along the bottom of one of the beech-covered hills that enclosed the north side of Edgewater.

They were nearly there when General Schofield said, 'I wish I could have persuaded Oliver to come with us. I think it would be a good thing for the whole family to get together and talk over what's happened. Not that I'm exactly family, but I'm the twins' godfather and they treat me as a sort of uncle. They call me Uncle Arthur. But understandably, I suppose, Oliver wanted to be left alone with Celia. She was there with him when I arrived. I asked both of them what they'd been doing about two o'clock yesterday, which was impertinence, perhaps, but I was fairly sure Dalling would have asked them that already and I wanted to know what they'd told him.'

'And did they tell you?' Sara asked.

'Yes, quite willingly. They said they'd been in the College canteen together. But they weren't sure if anyone there would remember them. They'd only helped themselves to sandwiches and cups of tea and hadn't talked to anyone else. Then Celia went to her lab, and Oliver went home. He didn't see his mother. He assumed she was having her usual rest. And after having put a few things ready for the party in the evening, he went up to see you to invite you to it. All as one would have expected, in fact, all a bit vague, nothing very definite, which I find much more convincing than an exact, careful, step-by-step description of what they'd done.'

'But the police suspicion that Mrs Cannon's death could have been murder,' Sara said, 'what did they say to that?'

'I think they were just bewildered. But they seemed just as bewildered by the possibility that it could have been suicide. They'd been sure yesterday Stamforth was mistaken about there being something wrong with the coffee and that it was a stroke that killed her. Of course, with the proof that she'd taken that drug it had to be suicide or murder, it couldn't possibly have been accident. If the quantity had been less it just might have been. She might have felt she needed a tranquillizer after getting as upset as she did about her birthday being ignored, as she thought it was being, and she might have unintentionally taken more than was safe. But even then, there's the question of how she could have got it—' He broke off. 'Now turn to the right here, then turn in at that gate on the left.'

Sara did as she was told. As she turned in at the gate of the farm drive she saw the house ahead of them, an old house, long and low, built of red brick, half-covered in dark weatherboards. The windows were small, with diamond panes, and there was an entrance in a low porch smothered in honeysuckle. There were hedges along the sides of the drive, with fields beyond them, brown after the harvest. A small red van stood in front of the house, with the words, 'Jos. Pringle, Builder and Plumber' painted in black on the side of it.

Sara drew up behind the van and she and General Schofield got out of the car and went up to the front door. They found it standing open and inside, at the bottom of a narrow, steep staircase, was a young man in a white overall on a stepladder. He appeared to be painting the ceiling. Hearing them come, he called out, 'Just a minute, I'm just done here—be with you in a moment.' And after a few more strokes with his brush over his head, he descended from the ladder and, carrying his can of paint and his paint-brush, came to the door.

'Are you Mr Pringle?' General Schofield asked.

'Is it him you want?' the young man asked. 'He's my dad.' He looked about twenty and was tall and broad-shouldered, with a large, amiable face and curly brown hair which hung about his shoulders. 'I'm on my own here today, just finishing the job. Thought I could get it all done yesterday morning, but with all these old beams it takes longer getting in and out among them than you'd think.'

'You were here yesterday morning, were you?' the General asked. 'I suppose you saw Mr Kimberley. It's him we want to see.'

'Can't say I actually saw him,' the young man said. 'They're harvesting up on the Ten Acre. He'd gone off there early before my dad and I got there. But I saw Mrs Kimberley and the kids, just before they went off to London. And she's in her studio now, I think, if you want her. But I think the kids are up with their dad on the Ten Acre.'

'She's in her studio, you say?' the General said, frowning slightly as if he were trying to think something out.

'That's out the back.'

'Yes, I know where it is. But you and your father got here yesterday before she left for London, did you?'

'Yes, she let us in.'

'Do you know about when that would have been?'

'Nine o'clock, as near as maybe. We generally tries to be punctual and she'd said specially would we be here by nine because she wanted to catch the nine-forty to London.'

'So you had the place more or less to yourself yesterday.'

'That's right, except I only stayed the morning and Dad went off after he was sure I could manage by myself. It's just that some of the plaster's been falling from the ceiling here in the hall and up the stairs, and we done the plastering the day before and come back yesterday to do the painting, only I didn't manage to finish as I'd got another job I'd got to go to in Bolding, so I come back again today.'

'I see. And about when did you go off to this other job yesterday?'

The boy grinned. 'D'you know, you sound just like the police? They been here this morning and asked me that very thing. I don't know what they were doing here, except that it's something to do with the death of that poor old lady in Edgewater who's Mrs Kimberley's aunt or something. "And what time did you leave?" they asked me, and, "You were here in the house all alone, were you, you didn't see Mr Kimberley?" And I said no, he was busy harvesting. You aren't police yourselves, by any chance?'

He seemed to have no objection to being questioned, in fact, rather to enjoy it.

'No, we're just friends of Mr and Mrs Kimberley's,' the General said. 'But did you tell the police when you went off to this other job?'

'Matter of fact, I went home first for my dinner,' the boy

answered. 'I dare say that would have been about half one. I made myself a cup of tea while I was here, because Mrs Kimberley said I could. We done lots of jobs for them here, you see, my dad and me, so we knows our way about, and Mrs Kimberley knows it's all right to leave us. Old houses like this, they're always needing little jobs done. Things keep falling to bits, like this plaster coming down.'

'And was there by any chance a telephone call while you were here?' the General asked.

It took Sara by surprise. She had not known what the General was aiming at in his questioning of the boy, except that she supposed he might be trying to find out if Ron Kimberley had an alibi. But she had not expected the telephone to be brought in. It made her look at the old man curiously, wondering if he was a good deal cleverer than she had realized, or if he had gone quite astray.

'No,' the boy said, 'not a telephone call. Well, that's to say . . .'

'Yes?'

'A wrong number there was, just before I left, say one o'clock. I heard it ring and keep on ringing, so after a bit I thought I'd better go and answer it, but when I spoke, just giving the number what's on the phone, whoever it was said, "Sorry, wrong number", and rang off. But there wasn't a proper call.'

'And did the police ask you if there was a call?'

'No, they didn't say nothing about that.'

Sara had an odd impression that the General was relieved. He gave a slight smile and said, 'Well, I think we'll go and look for Mrs Kimberley. I hope we haven't upset your work too much.'

'No, like I said, I was just finished.'

'Come along,' the General said to Sara, and retreated from the entrance and set off along a paved path that led round the house to the back where various barns and sheds surrounded what would once have been the old farmyard, but now was a neat patio with some garden chairs gathered round a small table on which there were some empty glasses and a bottle of whisky, looking as if they had been forgotten there from perhaps before lunch. From the fact that there were four glasses and that the twins did not yet drink, Sara deduced that the Kimberleys must have treated the two detectives to drinks while they were being interrogated, if something that could be called an interrogation had actually taken place.

'I suppose if I were to ask you what all those questions about a telephone call were about, you wouldn't tell me,' Sara said.

'Yes, yes, of course I'll tell you,' the General answered, but he sounded in a hurry. 'I'd like to talk to Meg first, however, and perhaps to Ron, if we can get him back from the Ten Acre. Odd how these fields keep their old names, isn't it, even though most of the hedges have gone and it's probably twice ten acres now? I do hope Meg won't mind our coming. She takes her work very seriously. Here we are.'

He approached the door of a fairly new-looking wooden shed and knocked on it.

A voice from within told them to come in. The General pushed the door open and he and Sara went into the shed. Sara saw Meg Kimberley stooping over a kind of wooden stand near a window through which a beam of sunlight shone, but the light in it was filled with floating motes of dust and Meg herself, who was wearing a loose green cotton dress, seemed to be almost screened by them. On the stand at which she was working there was a clay model of a galloping horse, not the kind of horse usually to be seen now taking young ladies for their riding lessons in files along busy roadways, but a creature with great flaring nostrils and flowing mane, mighty legs and hooves that seemed to be thundering across some empty plain. A Suffolk Punch, Sara thought, remembering pictures she had seen of those splendid animals in her childhood, though even then they had been made almost obsolete by the machine. There were other models of animals, mostly of horses, on shelves in the studio, some in cement and some in what she thought was bronze. She took only a quick glance round, but had a feeling that there was a rare vitality in all of them, a sense of life and movement, as there was in the creature under Meg's hands now.

'I'm afraid we're interrupting you, Meg,' the General said. 'Don't stop what you're doing for us. I only thought, in view of what's happened, it would be a good idea if we could all get together and have a talk. I'd have liked Oliver and Celia to come with us, but they wanted to be on their own.'

'Didn't you think of bringing Kay?' Meg asked. Her voice sounded dry and sardonic.

'Kay Eldridge?' For some reason the General looked embarrassed. 'I didn't think that was necessary.'

Meg gave a crooked grin. But she had hardly glanced up at him and Sara. Her large, intense, dark eyes were still on the horse on which she was working, and there was something remote about her whole attitude, as if she were only half-aware that anyone was there. The heavy fringe of dark hair that hung down over her forehead almost into her eyes was disordered, as if she had been thrusting her clay-covered fingers through it.

'Do you want to see Ron?' she asked. 'I'll go for him, if you like, but he'll probably be coming in soon for his cup of tea. Would you like some tea?' She reached down for a cloth that lay at her feet, soaked it in a bowl of water there and draped it over the horse. 'Let's go and sit outside.'

General Schofield had started wandering round the studio, looking at what was on the shelves. Standing still, he gazed with evident pleasure at a model of a mare with its foal.

'So you're working in bronze now,' he observed. 'I thought that was very expensive. Are you becoming so successful that you can afford it? Or was this commissioned?'

'No, and it isn't bronze,' she answered. 'It's *ciment-fondu*. A lot of trouble, but much cheaper, and it isn't a bad imitation of bronze to those who don't know better. I'm not making much money. And sculpture's really a very expensive occupation. I don't quite dare to call it my profession, you know, but I refuse to call it a hobby. And the fact is, Aunt Althea's money would have meant a great deal to us. Isn't that a fearful thing to say? There aren't many people I'd ever say it to. Naturally I didn't say it to the police.' She had finished arranging the wet cloth over the horse and was leading the way to the door. 'Do you know, we spent yesterday evening, after we got home, discussing whether or not we should sell the farm?'

Sara and the General followed her.

'Sell the farm—you don't mean that!' he exclaimed. 'Ron wouldn't think of it.'

She went over to the little round table and picked up the empty glasses there and the bottle of whisky.

'Oh, he's quite serious about it,' she said. 'He's been offered a rather good job with a firm called Bartle Waring who make and market agricultural machinery. Of course it would mean leaving Edgewater. Their main offices are in Reading. But they'd pay him a lot more than he's making out of the farm, and we could afford to keep the children at Granborough, which is one of our problems at the moment. If they'd go as day-children here of course we could manage it, but when that's suggested to them they say it would absolutely spoil everything. One gathers from them that the most important, or at least the most entertaining, part of their education takes place in the dormitories. Very wild things happen then that they wouldn't miss for anything.'

'Meg dear, I'd no idea things were as bad as that,' the General said. 'I could help, perhaps, anyway with the children's school fees. I've always intended—'

'Now don't let's talk about anything like that,' she broke in quickly. 'I didn't mean to start whining about our sad lot.' She turned to Sara and smiled at her for the first time. 'Sit down, won't you, Mrs Marriott, and I'll just take these things inside and bring out the tea.'

'Just a minute, Meg,' the General said, putting a hand on her arm. 'Before I forget, I want to ask you something. What train did you go to London by yesterday morning?'

She raised her eyebrows in surprise, so that they almost disappeared under her fringe of hair.

'That's just what the policeman wanted to know,' she said. 'He's quite sure, you know, that Aunt Althea was murdered, and he wanted my alibi. Could I possibly have been with her after she had lunch and dropped poison into her coffee? Actually I went up with the children on the nine-forty. We made a fairly early start so that we could be sure of getting home again in plenty of time for the party.'

'Did you go to the station by car, or on the bus?'

'By car, actually.'

'And you've still only one car, haven't you? And while you were in London—I know this will sound absurd—Jill didn't by any chance make a telephone call to anybody, did she?'

'Why ever should she do that?'

'I don't know. I just want to be sure she didn't.'

'Well, she didn't.'

He nodded his head, as if that only confirmed something that he already knew, but he was curiously careful not to meet Sara's eyes just then.

'Oh, here's Ron,' Meg said, looking towards the corner

of the house round which Ron Kimberley had just appeared with a twin on either side of him. 'I'll get that tea now, then we can all have that talk you want about our alibis and how none of us could have murdered Aunt Althea, because really it would be very difficult to prove that we hadn't the opposite of a motive.'

CHAPTER 6

She went into the house, carrying the bottle and glasses. The children, after greeting the General and Sara, followed her. Ron, Sara and the General sat down at the table. Ron's face and arms were looking even ruddier from the sun than they had the evening before. His fair hair looked bleached by it. Sprawling on his chair with his long legs thrust out before him, he said, 'The police have been here. I suppose you know that.'

The General nodded. 'They came to me too, before they came here.'

'For the same reason?' Ron asked. 'Did they want your alibi?'

'Yes, and they weren't too satisfied with the one I gave them. I told them I'd been at the luncheon of the Edgewater Historical Society at the Red Lion, and they seemed to think I could have slipped out of the crowd and cut across the road and dropped poison into Althea's coffee without its being noticed. Meg and the children of course were in London, but what about you, Ron?'

Ron Kimberley did not reply at once. He frowned, as if he were not sure how to reply, or perhaps simply in irritation at having been asked the question.

'So you were at the Red Lion,' he said.

'Yes.'

'And you go along with the idea that it was murder, do you?'

'I don't think one can simply dismiss it.'

'But the evidence they've got is so thin, they'd never prove it.'

'That's true.'

The two men seemed to be concentrating on one another in a way that Sara found strange. But so much that had been happening during the last day or two seemed strange.

'A book on the floor, for which there may be all kinds of explanations,' Ron said, 'and the puzzle of how Aunt Althea could have got hold of the drug. There may be all sorts of explanations of that too. Suppose someone who had access to a supply of the stuff got it for her, perhaps even being fairly sure that she meant to kill herself, would that be murder?'

'I suppose not, though it would probably be a crime of some sort,' the General said.

'I wonder if it's the kind of stuff one can buy in the streets, if you know where to go. Did Aunt Althea have any drug-pushers among her acquaintances?' Ron's tone was mocking.

'I should think the stuff almost certainly came from the College,' the General said. 'Anyway, that's what the police are going to investigate. And Oliver, of course, can come and go there and so can Celia and Kay. And you were a student there yourself once and know your way around. And you haven't answered my question, Ron. Where were you around two o'clock yesterday afternoon?'

Ron gave a tired-sounding laugh. 'You know, I believe you're enjoying this,' he said. 'Does it bring back old days? Weren't you in security for a time during your military career?'

'All right, if you don't want to answer . . .'

'Oh, I don't mind answering.' But Ron seemed to have

to consider what to say before he went on. 'I was up on the Ten Acre with Bob and Derek Charles—you know they're a couple of village lads who are working for me now—I was up there by six o'clock in the morning and I stayed there until—oh, I suppose it was about one o'clock when I came in to get myself some lunch. And as the harvest was virtually finished I left it to the boys and spent a couple of hours catching up on some office work I'd got behind with. It was hardly worth going back to the field because the boys could easily finish it. Then I had to wait until Meg and the kids got back from London and we could drive to the house with some stuff Meg had got ready for the party. I suppose it was about five o'clock when we got there. Does that tell you what you want to know?'

'More or less.' But the General did not look too certain.

'What's wrong with it?' Ron gave an ironic grin. 'I know you aren't satisfied.'

'There are just one or two things I'd like to ask you,' General Schofield said. 'When you got back to the house, was a boy working here, painting the ceiling in the hall?'

'Oh, young Pringle. No, he'd cleared off by then. I didn't even know till Meg got home and asked me if he'd finished the job that he was supposed to be coming.'

'And while you were having your lunch,' the General said, 'did you have a telephone call?'

Again Sara was taken by surprise at the General's interest in the telephone. It was as if he were looking for some connection between what she had told him about the call on her answerphone and some call that had been made to a real person.

Ron did not merely look surprised. His square, sunburnt face suddenly developed an alarmingly heavy scowl.

'And suppose I did, what has it to do with you?' he asked.

'I'm sorry, Ron. I didn't mean to interfere in your affairs,' the General said. 'I'm just trying to make sense of a rather odd thing that's happened. Don't answer if you don't want to.'

'Like hell you don't want to interfere!' Ron exclaimed. 'You've been trying to interfere ever since you found out about Kay and me. I suppose it was Meg who told you about it. And a lot she cares as long as she's left alone with her bloody horses. If you ask me, she's grateful because Kay has taken me off her hands. She doesn't have to worry about how I feel.'

'So you did have a call from Kay,' the General said peaceably.

Ron made an obvious effort to calm down and control his temper, but once more it took him a little while to decide how to reply. Then he gave another of his ironic smiles.

'Yes, I did, and I shouldn't have blown up when you asked me about it,' he said. 'I know everyone knows about Kay and me. Aunt Althea knew, did you know that? She had me in once and lectured me about it. If I thought the children were really upset, I suppose I'd put an end to it somehow. Yes, Kay rang me up to ask if I was sure it was all right for her to go to the party. Oliver had invited her and she'd agreed to go. But then she began to worry that Aunt Althea wouldn't really like her being there and I told her not to worry and go. That was all.'

'And about what time was that?'

Ron gave a puzzled shake of his head. 'I don't understand this. Why does it matter what time it was? Oh, I see! If I was here to answer it, it means I wasn't in town, poisoning Aunt Althea. Well, I didn't actually take any note of the time, but it was not long after I'd got in for lunch. That makes it around half past one perhaps. You can check with Kay.' He paused as Meg came out of the house with the children. She was carrying a tray on which there were cups and a teapot and a plate of sweet biscuits. He muttered, 'Can we talk about something else now?'

They talked about the fact that it looked as if the fine weather was breaking and that indeed it would not be surprising if it came to thunder soon. The air was as hot as ever, but there was a new heaviness about it and the sky had gradually been darkening, with clouds moving up across it in an ominous mass. Meg poured out the tea and Nick handed round the biscuits.

'I suppose you've been questioning Ron about his alibi,' Meg said with a smile that was not altogether agreeable. 'Did he satisfy you?'

'Look, can't we talk about something else?' he repeated, though it was plain from the way that he said it that he knew that she was aware of the telephone call from Kay Eldridge, which after all was his alibi.

'All right, suppose we talk about what we'd have done if we'd suddenly found today that we were wonderfully rich, instead of as poor as ever,' Meg said.

'What would we have done, Dad?' Jill asked, pushing most of a chocolate biscuit into her mouth. 'Would we have gone on a trip round the world? That's what I'd have liked to do.'

'And who'd have looked after the farm while we were away?' Ron asked. His manner had quite changed as soon as the children had appeared.

'Oh, we'd have sold the farm and bought a villa in Portugal,' Jill answered. 'That's what people do nowadays if they get rich. And they pay hardly any taxes. Did you know that? And Mum could have done all her work in bronze and become famous and Dad could have been just as lazy as he likes to be. That's what you really like, isn't it, Dad? I heard you and Mum talking last night and you said you wanted to sell the farm you were so fed up with it.'

'I'm afraid even if we did that, I shouldn't have much chance to be lazy,' Ron answered. 'I might even have to work harder than ever.'

'If we had lots of money,' Nick said, 'I'd buy a computer and a Rolls-Royce, and a sailing boat, and an answerphone—'

'A *what?*' the General interrupted.

'Just an answerphone,' Nick said. 'Everyone has them nowadays, I don't know why we haven't got one. And I'd move into a flat in London and Jill and I could go to the Royal Academy of Dramatic Art, then we could both of us get on to television and be important.'

'Do none of you really want to stay on the farm?' the General asked.

Meg laughed. 'I think they all over-estimate the extent of Aunt Althea's riches. Even if they'd come to us, we shouldn't have been able to do half the things they've been dreaming about.'

'And perhaps that's lucky,' Ron said.

She nodded. For once the two of them seemed to agree about something. 'The farm isn't such a bad place,' she said.

'Except that you hate it, don't you, Mum?' Jill said. 'I've heard you say so.'

'You shouldn't pay too much attention to the things I say,' Meg said. 'I get moods. There'd be times when I hated your villa in Portugal. Sara, some more tea?'

Sara had a second cup of tea and so did the General, and soon afterwards he said that it was time for him and Sara to be going. The family escorted them to the front of the house, where Sara had left the car, and stood in a group, waving to them as they drove off.

They were silent for a while until after they had left the farm behind them. It seemed to Sara that General Schofield was looking particularly thoughtful, as if he would sooner not talk, but there were certain things that she was determined to ask him.

Turning into the road towards Bolding, she said, 'You

said you'd tell me why you asked the Pringle boy all those questions about a telephone call. Why did you?'

'I'd have thought you'd have guessed that once you heard me ask Ron almost the same questions,' he said.

'I suppose I have, but I'd like to be sure about it. You were trying to find out if the message on my answerphone was somehow connected with the people here. From the things Ron said about the call he had from Kay Eldridge it almost sounds as if it could have been. I mean, what he said about what she'd said to him sounded almost exactly like what was on the tape. But that still doesn't make sense of the message to me.'

'No,' the General agreed.

'So what were you really trying to find out?'

He gave a sigh. 'I think there's going to be thunder,' he said.

A few drops of rain had just fallen on the windscreen and the clouds overhead were almost black.

'I suppose the fact is, you don't really know,' Sara said.

He smiled. 'That's just about right. That message to you worries me. It seems to me that for some peculiar reason it went to the wrong person and I'm just asking everybody I see if they've had telephone calls around one o'clock. I asked Oliver and I asked Celia and they both said no. And Ron says he did, and that doesn't make any more sense than if he'd said he didn't. The truth is, I'm just floundering around because I feel in my heart that that detective's right and Althea was murdered. And if she was, I want the person who did it caught. Only I don't think that's going to happen.'

'Why not?' Sara asked.

'Because they aren't even going to be able to prove that it was murder, not suicide. There's almost no evidence. There'll be an inquest and I imagine they'll return an open verdict, if they don't actually decide on suicide. But perhaps

if we could understand that call to you, we'd get somewhere. It's the one completely incongruous thing in all
that's happened.'

The rain was growing heavier and for a moment a flash
of lightning lit up the village of Bolding, then after a longish
interval there came a faint rumble of thunder.

'Ten,' Sara said.

'Eh?' the General inquired.

'I counted ten between the lightning and thunder,' Sara
said. 'I was taught when I was a child that if you did that
you could calculate how far away the storm was, and I
make this ten miles. But there's something else I want to
ask.'

'Yes.'

'About Kay Eldridge. Where does she fit into all these
things?'

'Ah yes.' But it sounded as if the thought of it depressed
him. 'I knew you'd get around to that sooner or later. Well,
I suppose it doesn't matter talking about it, since it's known
by everyone. There's no discretion left about such things.
She and Ron have been having a sort of on and off affair
for at least the last couple of years. I remember when it
began I took for granted he and Meg would be breaking
up, but then the thing seemed to come to an end and the
two of them just went on as if nothing had happened. So I
assumed then that the affair with Kay was over, but then
I was told by Oliver it had started up again and that Kay
was very unhappy because she'd believed Ron was going
to leave Meg and marry her. Kay's Oliver's secretary, you
know. But Ron didn't leave Meg. And to keep up with the
ups and downs of it all had been beyond me. I feel sorry
for Kay in a way, because I think she really believed Ron
was in love with her and was as serious as she was. I believe
the person who's called the other woman in that kind of

threesome often makes that mistake. She doesn't realize how strong the ties of a family can be.'

'And you think that's why he hasn't left Meg?' Sara said. 'The family.'

'I can't think of any other reason. I don't think, after the beginning, when I suppose they were in love after a fashion, that they've ever cared much for one another. You'd no children yourself, had you, to complicate your divorce when you'd made up your mind to it?'

'No, thank God,' Sara said. 'And is it because of the children that Meg stays with him?'

'Probably, though perhaps money enters into it. She hasn't any of her own and I don't suppose her sculptures will ever bring her much. So it may be convenient for her to be supported by Ron.'

A glaring flash of lightning lit up the road ahead of them and was followed almost immediately by a crash of thunder. Sara had not had time to count three between the two. Then it was as if the skies were suddenly emptied over them, the rain hammering on the car and spreading a flood of water over the road. For a moment she almost lost control of the car, feeling it skidding in what overflowed from the gutters. But then, leaning forward and with the windscreen-wipers swaying backwards and forwards in front of her, she managed to drive on. But she did not like inquiring further just then into the love-life of Kay Eldridge and Ron Kimberley.

However, a few minutes later, when the downpour had eased a little, though the thunder still seemed to be crashing directly above their heads, she observed, 'The voice on the tape could have been Kay's, you know.'

'Well, we know it wasn't Jill's,' the General said. 'That was one of the things I was trying to check with all my questions. In some ways it seemed obvious that it must have been hers. I mean, the easiest way to make sense of it was that it was a child playing a game. But if Meg took the children to London on the nine-forty, Jill couldn't have made a call to you after you'd left your flat at nearly ten o'clock, and Meg said she made no calls during the day. So if you think the voice could have been Kay's, perhaps you're right. You've heard her speak, have you?'

'Yes, at the party for Mrs Cannon. For a moment I was quite sure that it was she who'd spoken on the answerphone. But even if that's right, I still don't understand it.'

The thunder was moving away a little and a few minutes later Sara deposited General Schofield at his house in the High Street.

After she had done that she drove her car into the Cannons' garage and made a quick dash for the front door of the house, which as usual was standing open. The rain was still so heavy that even in that short distance she could feel it wetting her hair and penetrating the cotton blouse that she was wearing, even though the lightning and the thunder were less frequent. She let herself into the flat and saw with some dismay that she had left the two small windows in the sitting-room open and that the rain had been pouring in. Closing them, she fetched a cloth from the kitchen with which she could mop up the pool that had formed under each, then she dropped into a chair and sat staring vacantly before her, trying to remember everything that had happened that afternoon and to make up her mind how important any of it was to her.

For did it really make any difference to her whether Mrs Cannon had committed suicide, or been murdered? She had hardly known the woman. She hardly knew any of the people who were in any way connected with her. What was very apparent, however, was that General Schofield was most unlikely to continue working on his memoirs, at least until these questions had been settled to his satisfaction and that for Sara to remain in Edgewater would only be a waste of her time.

He might return to his project later, or for all she knew might abandon it altogether. It would be sad if he did, for she realized that she had been developing quite an affection for him. And when he had said that he had had an interesting life, he had not been exaggerating overmuch. She thought of what Ron Kimberley had said about the old man having worked in security during his career in the army. As far as he had gone at the moment in the story of his life he was still only at Sandhurst, with a certain young woman called Marie Landers beginning to form what sounded like an important relationship with him, and Sara knew that in fact two years later he had married her and they had gone out to Burma together. His work in security must have come much later than that, but meanwhile a war had been looming up, leading later for him to a Japanese prison camp, though his wife had escaped to Britain. He had eventually been one of the lucky ones to return home from the camp. But though Sara knew that much about him from odd remarks that he had dropped, these were not in a form that she could yet weave into a story. All the same, she had been becoming involved in her work and would have liked to go on with it.

Sighing because just for once when she felt this strongly, she also felt fairly sure that there would be no chance of doing so, she got up to help herself to sherry.

A few minutes later her doorbell rang.

When she opened the door she found Paul Fryer mounting the stairs. He had on an anorak with its hood up over his head, and although presumably he had only made a dash from his basement flat to the front door of the house its dark blue was spotted with rain. As she invited him in he shrugged it off and dropped it on a chair.

'Sherry?' she said.

'Thank you.' He waited until she had brought a glass to him, then went to a window and stood there, looking out. 'After all, you know, I'm going to be sorry to leave this place,' he said. 'I've done a bit too much roaming around in my life and for the first time I've felt settled here. But of course you won't be feeling like that. You've hardly had time.'

'Oddly enough, it's more or less what I was thinking about before you came.' She sat down in the chair where she had been sitting before his arrival. 'I don't mean about the flat itself, but that I'm almost sure my job with the General will be coming to an end and I've been getting quite fond of him. I'd like to stay. I feel curiously at home in Edgewater, I suppose because of the old days at Granborough. I've been out with the General to Bolding this afternoon and it brought back memories.'

He turned round to face her.

'What took you to Bolding?' he asked. 'Was it to visit the school?'

'No, it was to visit the Kimberleys.'

'Ah, detective work. And do you know any more than you did before?'

'I don't think so. But I've a feeling perhaps the General does, or thinks he does. I was only his chauffeur.'

'Does that mean he thinks Mrs Cannon's death was murder?'

'I'm inclined to think he does, though he didn't commit himself. What do you think yourself?'

'Oh, obviously murder,' he said, but he said it with mockery in his voice. 'Don't forget my trade. Suicide would make a very dull story.' He sat down on a sofa near her. 'What would you say to another meal at Pietro's?'

'Perhaps, if the rain eases up. If it doesn't, I could offer you some splendid frozen chicken pie.'

'I'd settle for that gratefully.'

'But Paul, there's something I'd like to ask you.'

It was something that had been on her mind for most of the day, though she had not seen herself asking him about it. But now with him sitting there before her with his curly black hair, his thick spectacles and his big, comfortable presence, she suddenly felt that it would be a very easy and sensible thing to do.

'Yes?' he said.

'You know when we went to Pietro's, someone got in here and stole something.'

His eyebrows went up. 'Something valuable?'

'I don't know.'

He gave her a puzzled look. 'Something the last people had left behind in the flat? Was that it?'

'Just something rather peculiar. But what I've been thinking about is that whoever came in and took it must have known I wouldn't be here. And who could have known that?' Their eyes met in a long, disturbing look. 'You knew, Paul.'

She could see what she thought was amusement in the dark eyes behind the thick spectacles.

'And you think I tipped someone off so that they'd know the flat would be empty and they could get in and pinch something. You think I asked you out to get you out of the way.'

'You could have done it without knowing what they meant to do. Did you tell anyone I was going to be out?' She tried to sound as if it did not matter very much.

'How could I when I didn't even know if you'd come out with me? Oh, wait a minute . . . !' He looked abashed. 'Did I tell anyone you were going to be out? Not exactly. But when the police let us leave the Cannons' place Kay Eldridge came down with me to my flat and I asked her if she'd feel like going to Pietro's with me, but she said she wanted to go home. So I said that in that case I'd see if you felt like going. I did say that. So I suppose you could say that Kay could have made a fair guess that you might go out. But for heaven's sake, Sara, Kay isn't a thief. I wish you'd tell me what was taken.'

She gave a sigh. 'All right, I'll try to, but it's such a weird story, and I've told it twice today already, to General Schofield and the police, and that hasn't got me anywhere, so I'm rather tired of trying to explain it.'

'You say you don't know if the thing was valuable.'

'I suppose it must have been to somebody, and for various reasons it's beginning to look as if it may have been Kay Eldridge.'

'Well, go ahead.'

For the third time that day Sara told the story of the nonsensical message that she had found on the tape of the answerphone and of its later disappearance. She also told Paul of her suspicions of Jill, but how she had definitely been cleared of having anything to do with it, and how, on hearing Kay's voice in the Cannons' drawing-room, Sara had thought that that might have been the voice that she had heard on the tape.

When she had finished he remained silent for a little while, thinking over what she had said.

Then he said, 'I know what it sounds like to me, but I can't think why the message should have come to you.'

'What do you think it sounds like?' she asked.

'As if Kay—no, we'll only say for the moment perhaps it was Kay—was talking on the telephone where someone could overhear her. She wanted to be overheard. She wanted someone, we don't know who, to think she was chatting to someone, probably Ron Kimberley, in a casual, affectionate way. You know about Kay and Ron, do you?'

'The General told me something about it,' she answered. 'He said everyone knew about it.'

'Everyone in the Cannons' and the Kimberleys' circle—
yes, that's probably true. In fact, not long ago we were all
expecting to hear that the Kimberleys' marriage had broken
up, and when that didn't happen I think we rather expected
Kay to start looking for a job elsewhere. But that didn't
happen either. And this message you had . . .'

'Yes?' she said as he hesitated.

'Doesn't it sound as if she wanted someone to believe
that she was on the same loving terms as ever with Ron,
although in fact she wasn't talking to anybody? I don't
know why she should do such a thing, but doesn't it sound
as if it was what must have happened?'

'But according to Ron himself, she did call him in the
afternoon and say to him almost the very things that were
on the tape.'

'He told you that?'

'Yes, when I drove the General out to see the Kimberleys.'

Paul shook his head. 'Then I don't understand it at all.'

'And then, you see, stealing the tape . . .'

'Could what she said on the tape have been a kind of
rehearsal for what she meant to say to Ron presently? No,
that really doesn't make sense. But I still feel the call you
got here was made on purpose for it to be overheard by
someone. I could go over to the College tomorrow and nose
around and see if I can find anyone who heard it. That
might be worth trying.'

'Paul, you're a biologist, aren't you?'

The sudden change of subject seemed to startle him. 'Of
a sort,' he said with a wry smile. 'I didn't get very far with
it. Why?'

'I was wondering if you know if they'd have a supply of
barbiturates at the College.'

'I dare say they would.'

'What for?'

He rubbed his forehead with a knuckle, as if that might help him to think.

'You're thinking, of course, of where Mrs Cannon or her murderer could have got the stuff from, and the College is the obvious place. I expect the police have already been going into that fairly thoroughly.'

'Yes, but why would they have it at the College? It's used as a sleeping-pill, isn't it?'

'That's one of its uses, though it's out of fashion for that. But trying to remember the little I managed to learn when I was working for my degree, I think it's used in preparing buffers.'

'What?'

'Buffers. Solutions in which acidity is stabilized.'

'Oh.'

He grinned. 'That doesn't tell you much?'

She finished her sherry. 'I don't know what it's like these days, but I'm afraid in my time the teaching of science at Granborough was a very hit or miss affair. You could go in for lots of it if you were that way inclined, or you could go and sit in the library and read thrillers if you'd sooner do that. Nobody seemed to worry much which you did. Have they got your books in the library, Paul?'

'As a matter of fact, they have, though I don't know if they get read by even as many as attend my stirring lessons.'

'But even if I don't in the least understand about those buffers, you've told me what I wanted to know.'

'That there's a legitimate reason for keeping a supply of barbiturates in the College, and so Oliver and Celia, both of whom work there, and Kay too, and even Ron, who was a student there, I believe, and probably still knows his way around, would have known how to lay their hands on the stuff.'

'I notice you're leaving yourself out,' she said. 'But you've that degree in biology and you know about buffers.

You'd have been able to recognize the bottle or the jar or whatever it is they keep the stuff in. And you did tell Kay this flat would be empty yesterday evening. What about it, Paul?'

He met her gaze, then finished his sherry, put the glass down, stood up, took hold of her hands and hauled her to her feet, drawing her close to him. The kiss he gave her was long and gentle. It was a long time since anyone had kissed her like that and as she let it happen and then began to respond to it, something that seemed hard and unbreakable in her melted away. When he held her a little away from him but she was still tight in his arms, she felt a little dizzy, but strangely like something that she had felt very long ago.

'I could knock you over backwards, if you like, like that first boyfriend of yours,' he said. 'Would that help?'

His voice was not as steady as he meant it to be.

'Sometime, perhaps. Not now,' she answered. 'There's that frozen chicken pie to attend to.'

'Ah, that's wonderful. Frozen chicken pie. Absolutely my favourite thing.'

She leant forward and this time it was she who kissed him, and it became not quite so gentle and lasted longer than before. Then she jerked herself free and went to find the pie in the refrigerator as if it were all that she could think about. She switched on the oven, waiting for it to heat before she put the pie into it. Then she refilled their glasses.

'And now we aren't going to talk any more about that wretched tape,' she said. 'I've had enough of it. Tell me about where you grew up.'

Sitting down with his glass, he said, 'It was in Devonshire. It was near Sidmouth.'

'And there were five of you, you told me.'

'Yes. I was number three in the family. There were three boys and two girls.'

'And what did your father do?'

'He was a solicitor. And I went to the local school and then somehow got to Cambridge.'

'And what about the other boys and the two girls? What's happened to all of them?'

He gave a laugh and said, 'That's what you really want to know?'

'Yes, for now. I'd like to be very calm and normal about everything. It's been such a terrible day.'

'Well, my elder brother's a solicitor too, in the family firm, and he's married and has three children. And one of my sisters is married and lives in Scotland, where her husband's a lecturer in Edinburgh University, and the other's still at school.'

'And what about your other brother?'

'Oh—he's got a job abroad.'

For some reason, it was obvious, he did not want to talk about that brother, and he went on then to ask questions about her family and presently she put the chicken pie in the oven and made a salad to go with it and when it was ready she put it on a tray and brought it into the sitting-room. They ate it with the plates on their knees in a quiet that she knew was artificial yet which gave her something for which she had been longing, she had not known how deeply. It gave her deep satisfaction to see his curly black hair, his sturdy build and the kind eyes behind the thick spectacles.

The rain still beat against the window-panes though the thunderstorm had travelled away. Presently he put on his anorak, pulled the hood up over his head and said that he had better go and he did not kiss her again. She stood on the landing, watching as he went down the stairs, then went back into the flat, closed the door, and remembered to lock it. She washed up the plates and glasses that they had used and as she did so caught herself singing an old song that she had learnt at school.

'"And indeed, sir, it's true, sir,
"I never was given to lie,
"And if you'd been to Derby, sir,
"You'd have seen it as well as I . . ."'

'The Derby Ram', of course. But she did not know why she was singing it, except that she felt like singing something. And someone had been lying about the nonsense on the tape, hadn't they? That could not simply be put out of her mind.

She had just put the crockery away in its cupboard when the telephone rang. She thought that it was probably Paul telephoning, perhaps to suggest that he might return to the flat, and she hoped it was, but it was the General.

'Sara, I've been doing some thinking, and I believe I may have an explanation of that message on your answerphone and why it got stolen,' he said. 'I can't swear I've got it right, but I believe I have. You'll be coming to see me tomorrow morning, won't you?'

'Yes, of course,' she said.

'I don't know if I'm going to feel like doing any work. I may give up the whole idea of my memoirs for the present. It's somehow come to feel a pretty foolish idea. But all the same, I'd be glad if you'd come. Of course, even if I give it up, I'll make sure you're paid for your time, so don't worry about that.'

'Could you tell me what your idea is?' she asked.

'It would be a bit complicated to talk it over on the telephone,' he said. 'But I'll tell you in the morning.'

'Then I'll be there as usual at ten o'clock.'

'Good. Good night.'

'Good night.'

She put the telephone down.

But although Sara arrived at General Schofield's house in the High Street at ten o'clock the next morning, he did

not tell her about the idea that he had had about the tape
on her answerphone. He did not come to open the door as
he usually did when she rang the bell. But then she found
that the door was unlocked and, pushing it open, she went
into his square, brown sitting-room. He was sitting in one
of the red leather chairs and staring at her with wide-open,
expressionless eyes. The colour of his face was a yellowish
grey, but the colour of his shirt was a dark, sticky-looking
red which must have gushed out from the deep wound in
his throat. A knife had been driven deep into it.

CHAPTER 7

The telephone was in the hall. As Sara dialled she leant
against the wall because she felt as if she might fall down
if she had nothing to support her. When she had spoken to
Detective-Inspector Dalling she dropped the telephone and
had to reach for it to put it back on its stand. Then she
stayed where she was for more than a minute, her breath
coming unevenly. She looked at the front door and thought
of letting herself out of the house and waiting on the pavement for the police to arrive. But she knew that that would
be foolish. In the end she went to the foot of the narrow
staircase that led up out of the hall and sat down on a step
near the bottom. Leaning her elbows on her knees, she held
her face in her hands, keeping her gaze steadily on the
door before her, as if that would make the men she had
summoned arrive more quickly. But when the door was
suddenly pushed open she nearly screamed. Then when she
tried to stand up to meet them she felt as if her legs might
buckle under her and she ended by staying where she was,
looking white but quite falsely calm.

Dalling came first, followed by Miller and with two

uniformed men behind them. She had heard the wailing of the police car sirens as they approached, and during the time that the door had stood open had seen two cars pull up opposite the house and curious passers-by already beginning to collect, looking up at it and even trying to peer in at the tall windows that overlooked the street. The men all went straight into the sitting-room after Dalling had given her one quick look and she had nodded towards its door. One of the uniformed men came out again almost immediately and went out to one of the cars and Sara saw him say something that looked angry to the knot of people outside, for they began to move off, though only a little way. Then he seemed to be speaking on a radio in one of the cars, then returned and went back into the sitting-room. After what seemed like a long time, Dalling came out and held out a hand to her, drawing her to her feet. He led her into the dining-room, a room that faced the one where Sara had always worked across the small hall. Like the other room, it was square and brown except for a portrait of a smiling woman that hung above the fireplace. But even the portrait was mostly brown in tone, though the eyes that looked out amusedly from under delicately arched brows were a gleaming grey. Sara guessed that it was a portrait of the woman who had been Marie Landers. Dalling guided Sara to a chair at the mahogany table and looked round the room.

'Brandy,' he said and started opening the cupboard doors in the mahogany sideboard. 'We could do with some brandy.'

He found a bottle in one of the cupboards and a glass and filled it and pushed it towards Sara.

'Drink it up,' he said. 'It'll help.'

She picked it up and sipped, then put it down again.

'I don't really want it,' she said. 'I just want to tell you—'

'Drink it up,' he interrupted. 'You need it. Then we can talk.'

He did not pour out a drink for himself, but pulled out one of the chairs from the table and sat down at the head of it. The dark eyes under his craggy eyebrows looked at her with a good deal of sympathy. Sara remembered that General Schofield had said of him that he was tactful and kind. But the thin lips of his mouth were pressed tightly together in a way that suggested a cold determination, rather than tact or kindness. It was almost as if there were two halves to his face which did not quite fit together.

When she had drunk about half of the brandy in the glass and was finding that it steadied her more than she had expected, she put the glass down, drew a sharp breath and said, 'Well?'

'Well,' he said, 'what is it you're going to tell me?'

'Where d'you want me to begin?' she asked. 'With how I got here this morning and found . . . ?' She had to stop because she realized that she was going to sob. It was not only that this was her first encounter with violent death, but that the brandy seemed somehow to have released in her a wave of affection for the old man. She had not known that she could grow to feel so much for anyone in such a short time.

'Go on, cry if you want to,' Dalling said. 'I'm used to it and it may do you good.'

'About my coming here this morning,' she said, 'you know I've been working here.'

'Working on a book with General Schofield, yes,' Dalling said. 'You told us about that.'

'Yes, his memoirs. It was very interesting. He'd had a very interesting life.'

'I've had an interesting life myself,' Dalling said. 'Perhaps I'll write my memoirs when I retire. Oh, I said that to you before, didn't I? Perhaps people are always saying it to you. So you came here as usual and how did you get in?'

'I rang the bell as usual, but no one answered it. Then I found the door was unlocked and I came in and went to that room across there and found—and found—'

The sob came this time and with it a gush of tears.

He did not try to hurry her, but when she had found her handkerchief and had mopped her eyes, he said, 'What time was that?'

'Just about ten o'clock,' she said. 'That was my usual time for coming.'

'So you telephoned us at once.'

'Yes, of course.'

'When did you see him last—alive?'

'Yesterday afternoon,' she said. 'I drove him out to the Kimberley farm. He wanted to talk to the Kimberleys. Then I drove him home. We started off just before the storm began and the rain was still pouring down when I put him down here.'

'Did you come in with him?'

'No.'

'And you don't know of anyone else who may have been waiting for him or come in later?'

'No.'

'It's just that there are a number of muddy footmarks on the carpets which don't fit his own feet.'

'I don't know anything about that. But there's something I ought to tell you . . .'

'Yes?' he said as she paused to dab at a tear that was trickling down her cheek.

'He telephoned me yesterday evening. Do you remember what I told you about that message that was left on my answerphone which sounded like one half of a conversation?'

'Yes, certainly.'

'Well, he said he'd had an idea about it and that he'd tell me what it was when I came here this morning. He said it was too complicated to talk about on the telephone.'

'He didn't give you any indication of what it was?'

'No.'

'It may be important.'

'That's how I feel myself, though I don't understand it. But there's something about our trip out to the Kimberleys that perhaps I ought to tell you, because it seems somehow to be connected with that message. He questioned Mr Kimberley about where he'd been the day before, around the time that Mrs Cannon must have got the drug in her coffee. And Mr Kimberley said he'd been out at the farm, having lunch and then doing some office work, and that he'd had a telephone call from Miss Eldridge—Miss Kay Eldridge—asking him if he was sure that it would be all right for her to go to Mrs Cannon's party. In fact, her call, according to him, sounded very like what was said on the tape that somebody stole from me. And the fact is that what I remember of the voice on the tape was very like Miss Eldridge's, though of course I can't say for certain it was hers.'

He nodded thoughtfully as he considered the possible implications of what she had said.

'It appears to be fairly well known,' he said after a little, 'that Mr Kimberley and Miss Eldridge have had an affair going for some time. In a way it's surprising that Mrs Cannon was ready to have her as a guest.'

'But perhaps she didn't know she'd be there. It was a surprise party. She won't have had anything to do with who was invited.'

'That's true. All the same, in his place I don't think I'd have risked asking Miss Eldridge. From what I've been able to learn of Mrs Cannon, she'd have been perfectly capable of turning Miss Eldridge out of the house, even if she was there as a guest. But perhaps she wouldn't have done that with Mrs Kimberley there. It might only have been painful and embarrassing for her. Did General Schofield talk at all to Mrs Kimberley while you were out at the farm?'

'Yes, in her studio. And she told him that only the evening before she and her husband had been discussing selling the farm and his taking up some job in Reading, because, apart from anything else, they weren't making enough money to keep the children at Granborough, at least as boarders, and the twins were awfully upset at the idea that they might have to become day-children.'

He nodded again. 'Of course places like that eat up money. And there's a perfectly good comprehensive in Edgewater, but I suppose that wouldn't be good enough for them.'

'I was at Granborough myself when I was a child,' Sara said, 'and I know it was very expensive, but I think that once children have got used to the rather eccentric sort of place it is, it really would be very difficult for them to adjust to something more conventional, at least while they were quite young. I remember I'd got pretty tired of it by the time I was sixteen and when I was sent to an awfully strict sort of place abroad I rather enjoyed it, it was such a contrast.'

'And how did Mrs Kimberley herself seem to feel about the idea of selling up and moving into a town like Reading?'

Sara tried to recall what her impression of Meg Kimberley had been.

'I don't think she really cared much, one way or the other,' she said. 'As long as she had her studio and some hope of making a success with her sculpture, I don't think she minded where she was. I doubt if she even minded about Kay Eldridge.'

'We'll have to talk to Miss Eldridge about that telephone call she made to the farm,' he said. 'Now it might be best if you went home. I'd like to talk to you again, but there's a lot to be done here first and you can't help any more just now. Do you feel all right to go home, or shall I send someone with you?'

Sara stood up. Her legs did not feel entirely under control and curiously as if there were liquid where there ought to have been muscle. But they obeyed her when she tried to move.

'I'll be all right, thank you,' she said.

'And we'll find you in your flat later?'

'If that's what you want.'

He put a hand under her elbow and saw her out of the house on to the pavement.

The police cars were still there and so was the crowd, though a constable was keeping them at some distance from the door, and when, on seeing Sara emerge, they showed signs of surging forward he thrust himself between them and her. He then asked her where she wanted to go and as she pointed to the house at the end of the street he went the short distance to it with her, so she had her escort after all. The front door of the house, as usual, was open, and Mrs Worth was standing in the doorway.

She was in her black trousers and a bright emerald green shirt, and was holding a duster and a tin of furniture polish. Her eyes were bright with excitement.

'It's true, is it?' she gasped as the constable turned away and set off up the High Street. 'That good old man— they've killed him?'

'Yes, it's true,' Sara said wearily.

'Mr Oliver saw the crowd collecting and the police cars and he went along to find out what it was, and that was what he was told. Oh, isn't it awful?'

'Yes, it's awful.'

Mrs Worth stood aside so that Sara could enter, but she seemed reluctant to abandon her good view of the street.

But when Sara started up the stairs, she followed her.

'I can come in this morning and do for you, if you like,' she said. 'I've been in and done Mrs Cannon's as usual, but I'm not wanted there to get the lunch as I always did before, because Miss Hancock's there and she says she'll get it. She was there already when I arrived and the way it looks to me is that she's moved in. So I've got the rest of the morning free.'

Sara's inclination was to say that she did not think it mattered if nobody cleaned her flat as she would be moving out of it perhaps that very day, or in any case very soon. But Mrs Worth was at her heels and it seemed to need more effort to tell her that she was not wanted than to let her into the flat.

'But how did they find him?' Mrs Worth asked. 'It isn't one of Mr Dickman's days for going.'

Sara supposed that Mr Dickman must be the little elderly man who cleaned the General's house for him.

'I found him,' she said.

Mrs Worth gave a little scream of horror.

'You poor thing, no wonder you don't look yourself! I'll tell you what I'll do,' she said, 'I'll get you a cup of tea.'

'No, please don't trouble,' Sara said. After the brandy tea had not much attraction.

'It's no trouble, dear,' Mrs Worth said, 'and it's what you need. You just sit down and I won't be a minute.'

Sara sat down in her usual chair by one of the windows and Mrs Worth disappeared into the kitchen. She was back in a short time with two cups of tea on a tray and a cigarette between her lips. She sat down on a chair near Sara's and said, 'Sugar?'

'No, thank you,' Sara said.

Mrs Worth helped herself to two teaspoonfuls of it. 'You're looking terrible, you poor thing,' she said. 'You mean you just went in and found him? And you knew right off he was dead?'

'There couldn't have been any doubt of it,' Sara answered.

'Yes, but how? I mean, how had they done it?'

'I'm not really quite sure.' Sara ignored the cup of tea that had been put down on a table at her elbow. 'I just saw he was dead and I went and phoned the police at once. I didn't stay to examine him.'

'But I mean, was he strangled, or stabbed, or shot, or what?' The excitement still glittered in Mrs Worth's eyes. 'Didn't you even see that?'

'He was stabbed,' Sara said.

'Not poisoned?'

'Perhaps he was poisoned as well as stabbed, I don't know. That wouldn't show, would it? But I think he was just stabbed in the throat. There was a lot of blood.'

'Now do drink your tea while it's hot,' Mrs Worth said. 'And it would do you more good if you'd have a good deal of sugar in it. Hot sweet tea for shock, that's what I was taught in the first aid classes I used to go to. He was such a fine old man, wasn't he?'

Sara began obediently to sip the tea, though she resisted the insistence on sugar.

'Yes, I'd got very fond of him,' she said.

'It kind of makes it look as if Mrs Cannon must have been murdered too, doesn't it?' Mrs Worth said. 'I mean, if General Schofield knew who done it and threatened whoever it was with telling the police, that would explain why he was killed, wouldn't it?'

'I suppose it would.' A fearful tiredness had taken possession of Sara and it seemed to demand less of her to agree with everything that Mrs Worth said than to try to discuss it.

'I think that's why it happened and I've got my idea who

done it, though it wouldn't be right to say when it's no more than a guess, would it?' Mrs Worth drew deeply on her cigarette. 'But I've been expecting trouble sooner or later, isn't that strange?'

'An intuition?' Sara asked without much interest.

'Oh, a bit more than that, though I never thought of it touching the poor General. But I told Mrs Cannon myself she was taking a big risk having the man here after what I found out what I did about him.'

'What man?' Sara asked.

'Why, Mr Fryer, of course,' Mrs Worth said. 'What I found out—but I wasn't snooping, mind, the thing was just laying there on the table and I was going to put it with his other papers when I saw the prison mentioned in it—so I thought I ought to look at it more careful and there it was as plain as could be. And then I told Mrs Cannon about it and she spoke to Mr Fryer, so she told me, and said I wasn't to say anything about it to anyone else. But after that he'd always do anything she told him. Shopped for her, mended a light that got broken, even decorated a room for her without charging anything. Well, it kind of stares you in the face, doesn't it?'

'You mean she was blackmailing him for something?' Sara remembered that Oliver Cannon had warned her that if she had any dark secrets she should be careful to keep them well hidden from Mrs Worth.

'That isn't a nice name for it,' Mrs Worth said, 'but yes, it must have been something like that.'

'You don't think it was just good nature on his part?'

Mrs Worth made a derisive sound.

'But what was this thing you found out?' Sara asked.

'Why, that he'd a brother in prison for dealing in drugs,' Mrs Worth replied. 'And it's my opinion that that's where Mr Fryer ought to be too because you can be sure he knew how to get the drug that killed Mrs Cannon. Either got it

for her, because, poor soul, she asked him for it, or gave it
to her one day in her coffee because he was tired of being
in her power. And she told the General what she knew
about him and the General let Mr Fryer know he knew all
about him, so now he's dead. That's a bit more than what
you call intuition, isn't it?'

Sara leant back in her chair and closed her eyes. She wanted
to blot out Mrs Worth. She wanted not to see her, not to
hear her voice, not to think about what she had said. She
wanted to blot out everything that had happened that
morning. Perhaps Mrs Worth understood this, for after a
few minutes she picked up the tea-tray and carried it out
to the kitchen, then the hum of the vacuum cleaner began.
She stayed for about an hour, washing the kitchen floor,
dusting and polishing, then coming to see Sara, patting her
gently on the shoulder and saying that she was going. Sara
struggled out of what had become almost a coma to reach
for her handbag and pay her for her work.

'You poor dear,' Mrs Worth said. 'But you'll feel better
by and by. Just take care now.'

She accepted her money and left. Sara sank back in her
chair and wondered when the police would come to talk to
her, as Detective-Inspector Dalling had said they would.
Meanwhile it felt impossible to settle down even to reading
the newspaper that had been delivered that morning. She
was glad when at last her doorbell was rung and she could
go to let them in.

But is was not the police who came up the stairs, it was
Oliver Cannon and Celia Hancock.

'Can we come in?' Oliver asked. 'There are some things
we'd like to ask you.'

Sara would have liked to tell them to go away, but she
recognized that as the person who had discovered the murder that morning she had obligations of a kind to other

people who had not been so unfortunate, if they at least had good reason to want to know what she could tell them. She let them both into the flat and Celia, as she came in, put an arm round Sara's shoulders and gave her a kiss on the cheek. She gave her odd smile which seemed to make her lips curve downwards rather than upwards. Her almost triangular face was very pale.

'The police were in to see us a little while ago,' Oliver said. 'I'd been up to the General's house when I saw them there and the crowd collecting, and they told me then what had happened, but it was only when the man Miller came in a short time ago that we heard it was you who had found him. It must have been a fearful experience. I wish we'd been able to help.'

Sara gestured to chairs and the three of them sat down.

'I've been trying not to think about it,' she said, 'which probably isn't the most sensible thing to do. I suppose you think it's connected with the death of your mother.'

'It does seem probable, doesn't it?' His heavy-featured face was set in a frown which was almost a scowl, though the tone of his words had been friendly.

'And that her death definitely was murder, not suicide,' Sara said.

'Really I've thought so from the first,' he said, 'because I couldn't think how she could have got hold of the drug, though I know that's not much in the way of evidence.'

'But I told you how she could have done that,' Celia said in a slightly raised and petulant voice. 'I know it sounds unlikely, but it's perfectly possible. And it's possible that General Schofield's death had nothing to do with hers. It's got around that he was writing his memoirs and there may be people who are very frightened of what he might say. I know that sounds melodramatic, but I believe there's something in it, and if I were Sara I don't think I'd stay around in Edgewater any longer than I could help.'

'That's nonsense,' he said.

'Can you tell me how Mrs Cannon might have got hold of the barbiturate?' Sara asked.

Celia gave another of her peculiar smiles. 'Oliver won't listen to me, but I think it's perfectly possible. They have a Visitors' Day at the College during the summer term, and of course Oliver took his mother as a guest and showed her round the place. Actually he must have done that lots of times by now. And somehow, on one of those occasions, I believe she spotted where the barbiturates were kept and she went in quietly one day and helped herself to a good dose of the stuff. She was quite well known in the College and if anyone had seen her wandering about they'd only have thought she was looking for Oliver. Or perhaps she bribed one of the technicians to get it for her. That may be more likely. It may have been only a few days ago that she did it, or it may have been quite a long time back. We don't know how long she may have had the idea of suicide in her mind.'

'That's nonsense,' Oliver repeated with a surliness which was not often in his voice when he spoke to Celia. 'It wasn't suicide, and General Schofield wasn't killed because of anything he was going to write in his memoirs. Somehow he knew something about my mother's death. He may even have seen someone come into the house at the relevant time. He was at luncheon at the Red Lion that day and there's a window in the men's room there that looks straight out towards this house. He may have been in there and seen someone come, or perhaps leave, around two o'clock.'

'But his eyesight was poor, wasn't it?' Sara said.

'Was it?' Celia said. 'I always thought that for someone of his age it was marvellous.'

'Well, one of his reasons for asking me to drive him out to the Kimberley farm yesterday,' Sara said, 'was that he felt his eyesight wasn't to be trusted any more.'

Oliver nodded. 'Yes, I ought to have remembered that he'd almost given up driving because of his sight. But that doesn't mean he might not have been able to see someone come into or leave the house. He might not have been able to tell for sure who it was. Perhaps he might not even have been able to tell if it was a man or a woman, since we all dress alike nowadays. But he could have seen a figure there and something may have told him who it was. Or perhaps he said something that made whoever it was think he'd been recognized, even if he hadn't been. Of course it was someone whom my mother knew well.'

'Yes, that seems certain,' Celia said. 'If someone really put poison into the coffee she always made for herself after lunch, about which as you know I'm very doubtful, they'd either have had to be with her in the kitchen while she was making it, or have gone to sit with her in her bedroom when she went there to lie down and had the tray beside her bed. That does indicate someone she was fairly intimate with. But really I think it's more probable that she put the stuff in her coffee herself. That book being on the floor doesn't impress me. And I do think it's possible that the two deaths aren't connected.'

'All right, it's possible,' Oliver said, but he sounded unconvinced. 'Sara, what we really came up to ask you about is a message we've been told was left on your answerphone and then got spirited away. We don't quite understand it and we wondered if you'd mind telling us about it.'

'Who told you about it?' Sara asked.

'Paul Fryer,' he answered. 'But what he told us didn't seem to make sense.'

'I don't think it does make sense,' Sara said. 'An answerphone doesn't answer back, yet what I heard sounded just as if someone was having a conversation with someone else.'

She gave him a description of how she had found the message and what she could remember of what had been said, and then how the tape had vanished. But she found that she was feeling less and less trust in her own recollection of what had been said on it. It was as if what she thought that she remembered might be only what she herself had said of it and that this might have been distorted by repetition. She said nothing of thinking that the voice she had heard might have been Kay Eldridge's and when Oliver asked her if the voice had been at all familiar to her, she only gave a shake of her head.

'Is it possible, d'you think, that it was someone you know in London ringing you up as some kind of joke?' he asked. 'Do any of your friends know your number here?'

'I gave it to a few people the first day I moved in,' she said. 'But if I wanted to play a trick on somebody I'm sure I could think up something better than that.'

'Was your own name on the tape?' Celia asked.

'Oh yes.'

'Just what had you said?'

'I think I said, "This is Sara Marriott's number, but she is sorry she is unavailable. Please leave your message and your telephone number. She will call you as soon as she can." It was something like that.'

'You're sure of that? I mean, that your name was on the tape?'

'Quite sure.'

'It's just that I was wondering, you see, if it was possible that the message was really intended for the Marsdens by someone who didn't know they'd left.'

'I thought of that,' Sara said, 'but even if it was, it still doesn't make sense, does it?'

'Unless . . .' Celia paused and then to Sara's dismay she heard her own fanciful theory that the message had been in some kind of code being seriously suggested to her.

Oliver laughed, which obviously annoyed Celia. Her face lost the friendliness that it had had when she came into the room. Reaching out a hand and taking hold of one of hers, Oliver stood up and pulled her to her feet.

'You're too full of theories this morning,' he said, 'and I'm sure we've troubled Sara enough. It's time for us to go. Come along. And if we can help you in any way, Sara, let us know.'

Celia had stood up, but she resisted him when he drew her towards the door. 'There's just one thing . . .' she said.

Sara had stood up too. 'Yes?'

'There's no one but you who saw this mysterious tape, is there?' Celia said.

The implication was obvious, but Sara was careful to control the spark of anger that flared inside her.

'Only the thief,' she said.

'Ah yes, the thief.' Celia's tone was sceptical. 'What a pity there's no one else who knows anything about it. Well, we'll leave you in peace now. We'll be seeing more of the police presently, I imagine, but as Oliver said, do let us know if there's anything we can do to help.'

The two of them left then. As the door closed behind them the anger on which Sara had kept a tight hold while they were still in the room burst out of her, making her want to shout abuse after them, or even pick up the vase that still held General Schofield's gladioli and dash it on the floor. Not that she had anything against the vase or the gladioli, but simply to do something violent. When a normally truthful person finds her word doubted it can cause bitter rage. She is so used to having what she says accepted as a matter of course that she does not know in the least what to do about it. Why should Celia doubt her story about the answerphone? The police had not doubted it. But as that thought occurred to her it suddenly occurred to her to wonder if they really had believed her, but being professionals, had kept their doubts to themselves until it might be useful to show them.

With the seed of mistrust sown in her mind, she began to wonder if anyone had believed her. Had the General believed her? Had Paul Fryer? Only if she had had some mysterious reason for telling a lie, surely she could have thought of something better than that. That story as it stood was singularly pointless. As she turned that thought over in her mind, she began to calm down and settled back into her usual chair. One thing was obvious, she thought, and that was that Celia Hancock suspected that the man she was going to marry was the murderer.

Thinking about this possibility, Sara came to the conclusion that however mistaken Celia might be, she was suffering from a deep fear that Oliver had killed his mother and General Schofield. She had pointed out that Mrs Cannon might have been able to obtain some barbiturate at the Agricultural College and that she might have had the thought of suicide in her mind perhaps for a long time. She had insisted that the two deaths might not be connected and that the General had been murdered because of something that he was going to betray in his memoirs. She had first suggested that the message on the tape might be in code, and then that perhaps it had never existed at all, in other words that Sara might be a distinctly suspicious character. And what could the reason for all that be but an attempt to steer suspicion away from Oliver? Yet had not she herself given him an alibi for the time when the poison must have been put in Mrs Cannon's coffee? Was there something wrong with that alibi?

Then another thought came to Sara. Was it to steer suspicion away not from Oliver but from herself that Celia had put forward her suggestions? Had she murdered Mrs Cannon?

But surely the stabbing of General Schofield had been

done by a man. Was it possible after all that the two deaths were unconnected?

It was while she was turning this over in her mind that Sara's telephone rang. She reached for it and recited its number.

A familiar voice said, 'Sara? It's Miriam.' Miriam Bryanston was Sara's editor in London. 'I thought I'd ring up and ask how you're getting along with General Schofield. Were we right to take him on, or is there really nothing in it for us?'

'Then you haven't heard,' Sara said. 'No, you couldn't have yet. But it'll be on the one o'clock news.'

'What?' the other woman said. 'What's happened?'

'An awful thing, Miriam,' Sara answered. 'He's dead.'

'Dead? Oh dear, I'm sorry. But he was very old, wasn't he? I suppose we should have been prepared for it. I hope you hadn't put in too much work on his book. But I've got something else set up for you here, if you'd care to take it on. I was wondering who I could get to do it, but it would just suit you.'

'He was murdered, Miriam.'

'Murdered! No!'

'Yes, sometime last night. And I was the person who found the body in the morning.'

'Oh, Sara, oh, I'm so sorry. How frightful for you. How did it happen?'

'I don't think anyone knows much about that yet, except that someone got into the house somehow and stabbed him in the throat. For all I know, he let the person in himself. Anyway, when I went round to the house this morning the door was unlocked and I found him sitting in his usual chair, fully dressed, as if he hadn't been to bed. I've been asked a good many questions by the police, but I think there are probably more to come.'

'And haven't they any idea who did it?'

'If they have, they haven't told me.'

'So I don't suppose you know when you'll get back to London.'

'No, of course there'll be an inquest and I'll have to go to it, but I don't know when it'll be. And I don't know whether or not I'll just have to stay here, waiting for it, or if I can go to London in the meantime. I'm afraid I'm not thinking very clearly about anything just at present. I've never had a shock quite like it.'

'Do get here as soon as you can, because this thing I've got lined up for you should really interest you. It's the memoirs of Mary Markle. Does that mean anything to you?'

'It faintly rings a bell.'

'She's ninety-one and she's been married three times, the first time to a jockey, the second time to a ballet dancer who turned out to be homosexual but very well known in his day, and the third time to a professor of psychology somewhere or other. They're all dead, so we needn't worry about libel. And when she was about forty she began to write children's books with tremendous success, but then hers went out of fashion so she dropped it and took to dress-designing, which was successful too, and then a few years ago her books suddenly took off again and began to make her a lot of money on television—that's probably where you've heard of her and children adore them. Her central character's a mule called Montgomery who wishes he was a horse, but he's ever so much cleverer than all the horses he mixes with and he has a father who's a very wise old donkey—Sara, are you listening?'

'Trying to,' Sara said. 'But I told you, I'm a bit confused.'

'I think you'll find she's had a very interesting life.'

'Oh, all these people who've had interesting lives! I keep hearing about them.'

'What did you say?'

'Never mind. I'll think about it, Miriam, but at the moment I honestly can't promise anything.'

'Of course I understand that, but I'll do my best to keep her on ice for you, though ninety-one is perhaps a bit old for us to risk any delay. I mean, we don't want you wasted on another fatality.'

'Is she likely to get murdered, then?'

'No, no, I was thinking of that normal thing that comes to us all. Well, take care of yourself, my dear, and I'm really terribly sorry about everything and I wish I could help. Give me a ring soon to tell me how things are going. Nobody suspects you of anything, I hope.'

'I hope so too.' But even as she said it Sara's thoughts reverted to the question of what the police really believed about the message on her answerphone. Was it very naïve of her to think that anyone had believed her story of it?

At that moment her doorbell rang.

'Goodbye, Miriam,' she said. 'I must go. There's some-one at my door.'

'The police?'

'I imagine so.'

Putting the telephone down, she went to open the door.

CHAPTER 8

Again it was not the police. Two young men whom Sara had never seen before mounted to her landing. One of them had a camera and before she was aware of what he intended to do he had lifted it and taken a photograph of her.

'Thanks,' he said. 'That's fine.'

'You're Press, I suppose,' she said dubiously.

The other young man produced a card and held it out to her.

'The *Edgewater Advertiser*,' he said. 'My name's Norman Goode. I don't suppose the national press has got on to you yet, but they'll be along. And if you could tell us just a few things before they get here, we'd be very grateful. Your name now?'

She did not invite them into the flat, but she told them her name and said she supposed that besides working for the *Edgewater Advertiser* they were no doubt local representatives of one of the London newspapers. Norman Goode admitted that they were and went on to ask her if it were true that she had discovered the murder of General Schofield that morning, how she had done so, what her relationship with him had been and what her emotions had been on discovering the tragedy.

She thought that the swiftest way of getting rid of him was to answer his questions, though she did it as curtly as she could and would not admit to having had any emotions. He seemed very pleased, thanked her with a friendly smile, said, 'Come along, Pete,' to his companion and the two of them departed. She closed her door and resolved not to open it again until she was sure who was on the other side of it.

But what should she do about lunch, she wondered. She did not really want to eat, yet she felt a nervous sort of hunger. The old stand-by of bread and cheese, she thought, would really be best. Yet as she went out to the kitchen to fetch some from the fridge, she found herself wishing that someone else would call on her, even the Press. She would have welcomed the police because she could have asked them if they had discovered anything about the murder, but they did not appear. She felt, however, that she had to stay in the flat as she had told them that that was where they would find her when they wanted her, though as time passed she became restless and would have been glad of a chance to go out for a walk.

Yesterday's storm had passed and the day was fine. It was not as oppressive as it had been the day before. A faint breeze was blowing, sending small clouds scurrying across a pale blue sky. From her bedroom window which over-looked the High Street she saw that there were still police cars outside the General's house and that barriers had been set up, preventing the small crowd that still gathered about it from approaching too close to its door. It was nearly three o'clock before her doorbell rang again.

This time she went up to the door, put her head close to it and called out, 'Who's there?'

'Paul,' was the answer. 'Shall I come in or go away?'

She opened the door. He stood still for a moment, looking her up and down as if something about her appearance startled him, then he took her in his arms.

'God, you do look as if you've been through it,' he said. 'I only heard of it some minutes ago. I've been out all day. You know I'd have come here sooner if I'd known.'

Holding his arm, she drew him into the room and closed the door.

'Who told you about it all?' she asked.

'Mrs Worth,' he answered. 'She doesn't normally work here in the afternoons, but she doesn't seem able to tear herself away. She's been turning my place upside down as an excuse for staying.'

'She's been telling me some strange things about you,' Sara said. She went back to her chair and sat down and Paul stood in front of her, looking down at her.

'I think I can guess what they were,' he said. 'She's always taken a rather indecent interest in my affairs. It was about my brother, wasn't it?'

She nodded.

'Well, it's all quite true,' he said. 'Justin got in with a bad crowd when he was at the university, started to need money for the drugs he was taking and made it by pushing

them. Then things got worse and he took to stealing. He
and some friend of his broke into a house and went off with
all the money they could find, which was two or three
hundred pounds. But they were caught by a tough neighbour and arrested. Things might have been worse still,
because the friend had a gun on him, only luckily it was
unloaded and could only have been used for scaring anyone
they ran into. And they've both been in prison for a year
and will be coming out soon, and then the family has got
to decide what to do about Justin.'

'And Mrs Worth found this out and told Mrs Cannon?'
Sara said.

'Yes, but I'd already told Mrs Cannon myself,' he
answered. 'I'd been in the basement flat for about a year
when it happened and I told her about it straight away and
offered to move out if she felt there was anything disrepu-
table about me. And I told them at Granborough too and
offered to resign. But both said I should stay on. Mrs Worth
did find a letter in my flat from my solicitor brother which
explained how things were and told Mrs Cannon about it,
but she already knew the whole story by then.'

'Mrs Worth believes it's because Mrs Cannon knew your
secret and had power over you that you used to do all those
little jobs for her,' Sara said. 'And you see, if she'd been
blackmailing you into doing her shopping for her in the
supermarket, it would have given you a motive for her
murder, wouldn't it?'

He gave a rather sad laugh. 'Mrs Worth's a nice woman
really, you know, kind and helpful. And perhaps there's
some truth in what she said, if you slightly change the
emphasis. I thought Mrs Cannon was so good about the
whole thing that I really enjoyed doing anything I could
for her. But that wasn't exactly blackmail on her part. I
don't suppose she even realized how I felt.'

'And where have you been all day?' Sara asked.

He moved towards her, sat down on the arm of her chair and started to wind a finger in the curly hair on top of her head.

'Playing detective,' he answered.

'Something to do with my stolen tape?'

'Yes.'

'What have you been doing about it?'

'Thinking, mostly. But I went for a walk after breakfast, went off across the Heath, sat down on a bench by the river for quite a while, then decided what I'd do. I went to the College and went looking for Kay Eldridge.'

'The College is functioning, is it, although it's a vacation?'

'Oh yes, there are no students there, but research goes on. But I couldn't find Kay. I found the girl who shares an office with her, however, and that turned out to be very informative, more so, perhaps, than talking to Kay herself. The girl told me she wouldn't be coming in today because she'd a migraine.'

'What does this girl do at the College?'

'She's the secretary of the head of the chemistry department, and what she told me about was a telephone call that Kay made on the day Mrs Cannon died, just about lunch-time. Kay's own telephone was out of order, that's why she made the call from the office. She said Kay was in a rather odd state of mind, giggling a lot about nothing and then suddenly snatching up the telephone on her desk and dialling, and after a moment saying to someone, "Sorry, wrong number," and slamming it down and saying, "Damn!" Then apparently she took a little time to think about what to do next instead of simply dialling again, but then she did dial and started off saying, "Darling, it's me . . ." Then she went on chatting about a party she was going to and this girl I was talking to took for granted she was talking to Ron Kimberley, because everyone knows about Kay's affair with him. But it seems that although she appeared to be told that everything about the party was all right, she looked very worried, and then when the other girl asked her if she was coming along to lunch in the canteen, she only said, "Have I made a hell of a blunder?" and walked out of the room. And the girl said the police had been along to ask her about that call and she'd told them just what she'd told me and naturally she was so excited about it all that she wanted to go on and on talking about it, but that's really all the information she was able to give me.'

'And what do you make of it?' Sara asked.

He stood up and began to walk about the room, frowning down at the floor. 'I'm sure Kay's friend was meant to overhear that call,' he said. 'You see, if the truth had been that Kay was talking to Kimberley at the farm and he was answering her from there it would have given him an alibi for the time when the drug must have been put into Mrs Cannon's coffee. But for some reason she talked to your answerphone instead of to the farm, and I don't understand that.'

'But Ron Kimberley told the General he'd had the call at the farm,' Sara said. 'And in any case he'd never have had the time to get into Edgewater and back home during the afternoon, because Meg had taken the car to the station. He would have had a very long walk.'

'Well, did Kay ever call him, or had it merely been arranged between the two of them that he was to say he'd had the call, so that it would give him his alibi? Then he might have left the farm far earlier than he said.'

'Paul, you know what you're saying, don't you?'

He stood still and transferred his frowning look to her face.

'That Kimberley murdered his aunt—yes, I know I'm saying that, and he had about as little motive for doing that as anyone could have had. So I've gone wrong somewhere. And why the call to your number?'

'There's something I may not have told you,' Sara said, trying to remember just how completely she had told him all that had happened at the Kimberley farm. 'When General Schofield and I got to the farm a young man was doing some decorating in the hall, painting the ceiling. And he said he'd been there the day before but he hadn't seen Ron because presumably he was out harvesting in some field he called the Ten Acre. Then just before he left, he said, the telephone rang and he thought he'd better answer it, but whoever it was only said, "Sorry, wrong number," and rang off. And that might have been the wrong number Kay's friend heard her make, mightn't it?'

He nodded thoughtfully. 'I see. I think I do see something. Suppose Kay was to make that call to the farm in her friend's hearing and go ahead with her talk about the party, and if Kimberley wasn't there, there shouldn't have been any answer. Yet a man's voice did answer and Kay just rang off quickly and then wondered what on earth she was to do, because it was still important that her friend should hear her make the prearranged call, and her own phone, which she might have rung, was out of order. So she had the bright idea of calling your number, because she knew that the Marsdens had left and didn't know that you'd moved in. And I suppose she knew the Marsdens' number and could ring it straight away, and perhaps she was used to getting an answerphone if she dialled them and thought they'd accidentally left the thing on when they left and that it was safe to go ahead.'

'But wait a minute, Paul. My name was on that tape.'

'That complicates things. All the same, I think we're getting somewhere.'

Sara shook her head. 'Ron didn't murder his aunt. You don't murder someone to prevent them giving you money.'

'Certainly that seems unlikely.'

'And what did you do after you'd finished talking to Kay's friend?' she asked.

'Had lunch in the pub that's just beyond the College, and then I did something . . . But I'll tell you about that presently. Sara, you're sure your name was on that tape?'

'Quite sure,' she said.

'I suppose if Kay was flustered and confused by getting that answer from the farm when there shouldn't have been one, she might not have taken it in. And there's another thing that may have helped to confuse her. Your name's Sara Marriott, and the Marsdens' names were Sam and Harriet, so she might have misheard them. But of course after meeting you at the party and hearing that you'd moved into the flat she'd have realized what had happened and that she'd got to get the tape back, and when I told her I might be taking you out to Pietro's she thought it was safe for her to do it. Yes, don't you think that's how it must have been? She didn't know what she ought to do when she got that answer from the farm and she didn't really listen to the tape very carefully, but after she'd made the call she said she wondered if she'd made a hell of a blunder. Doesn't all this almost make sense?'

'Almost, Paul, yes. But not quite, does it?'

'Because of the missing motive. You're right, of course.' He reached for her hands and drew her to her feet. 'Could we forget all this for a little while?'

'I wish I could,' she answered, standing with her hands in his. 'But we haven't even begun to talk about the General.'

He let go of her. 'Yes, I'm a fool. I'm sorry. But Sara, I think I'm falling in love with you.'

'And what I feel is that I'm just falling, down and down, I don't know where. The picture of that old man with the knife sticking out of his throat . . . I see it all the time.'

'Shall we go to Pietro's presently?'

'I've told the police I'll be here till they want me.'

He muttered something derogatory about the police, then let her drop back into her chair. He stood at the window with his elbow on the window-sill.

'Shall I tell you where I went after I'd had my lunch in the pub?' he asked.

'Yes, do,' she said.

'I drove out to Granborough and handed in my resignation.'

'Oh, Paul, whatever made you do that?'

'It's something I've been on the edge of doing for some time,' he said. 'I'm not a born teacher and that's what you have to be to teach in a place like that. I really admire the people who can make a good job of it. And when I think of simply looking for a job in a more conventional place which wouldn't really make such big demands on one, the thought appals me. I believe when I first started working for my degree I thought I was going to turn into a notable scientist, but it didn't take long to cure me of that idea. All the same, I went on and got a top second and then there seemed to be nothing to do but teach. And I thought I was marvellously lucky to get a job at a place like Granborough and for a time I was honestly enthralled by it. But then I started to write in my spare time and teaching became more and more of a bore and I saw myself turning into the kind of person I've no use for, the mere dabbler and dilettante who can't make up his mind what to do with his life. And so at last I made up my mind and drove out to Bolding this afternoon and handed in my resignation.'

'But it's holidays, isn't it?' Sara said. 'Who did you hand it in to?'

'Oh, the administrative people are there and so's old Hamlyn himself. He's the present headmaster and he's rather a grand old boy. And I had a long talk with him and he told me he thought I was right to go if I felt as I did.

He doesn't want anyone around but the wholly dedicated. And we had a rather curious talk about the Kimberley twins. He knows I know the family and it was he who brought the matter up. He said he doesn't think Granborough's good for them and he thinks they'd be better off somewhere farther away from their family. Then I realized that that was what he was really worried about, not the effect of the school on them. They've a rather peculiar home, a mother who thinks of nothing but her sculpture and a father who simply flaunts his love-affairs in front of everyone, yet who's always hanging about the school, fussing over what the twins are doing and trying to push them out in front of the other kids. I've noticed that myself and naturally I've thought it was pretty bad for them. It doesn't make them particularly popular and so they tend to cling together even more than twins usually do.'

'Paul, you said just now that Ron Kimberley flaunts his love-affairs in front of everyone,' Sara said. 'You said it in the plural. Have there been others before Kay?'

'I'm afraid that was a slip of the tongue,' he answered. 'It wouldn't surprise me if there had been, but I don't know of anyone.'

'But when you leave Granborough and won't go and teach anywhere else, what are you going to live on?'

He laughed. 'It's probably rash and a bit vain, but I think I'm going to live on my writing. What made me act today was that I received a very nice contract in the post which I've been waiting for hopefully for the last few weeks, and there was a cheque too a few days ago from America which will keep me going for a while, and recently I've been getting odds and ends in the way of translations and one or two things on radio. But with that contract I know where I am for some time to come, if I can only keep on producing the stuff, and I feel fairly sure I can. And after all, I've no one dependent on me. If I come a cropper I'm the only one who'll suffer.'

'And that's why you don't mind giving up your flat when Oliver sells the house,' Sara said, 'or will you be staying in Edgewater?'

'No, I'm aiming at London, if I can find somewhere to live that I can afford. Do you think I'm an awful fool, Sara?' He turned towards her from the window.

'I'm not the best person to ask that sort of question of,' she replied. 'I haven't made such a success of my own life so far that I feel competent to give advice. But I think there's a possibility that you're being very wise. I wish you luck, anyway.'

'I'll have trouble with my family,' he said. 'They'll all say I'm crazy.'

'They've read what you've already written, I suppose.'

'I can't swear that they have. I think it happens quite often that the last people to take interest in what one's doing are the members of one's own family, and we happen to be a competitive lot and perhaps a bit jealous if one of us shows any signs of making a success of things. I've got to admit I haven't taken much interest in their various careers, except, of course, Justin's, and that hasn't been altogether voluntary. Now I'll be going, and you're coming out with me to Pietro's if the police don't come too late.'

He bent down and kissed her quickly, then let himself out.

As soon as he had gone she wished that he had stayed and thought of going out on to the staircase to call him back. But suddenly she was aware that she had never felt so tired in her life. Exhaustion, a sense of being emotionally utterly drained, kept her motionless and without even meaning to, she closed her eyes. In a few minutes she was fast asleep.

*

It was her doorbell ringing again that woke her and once more it was representatives of the Press. As before, she answered direct questions accurately but briefly. She spoke only of why she had gone to see General Schofield and her discovery of his death. She said nothing about the death of Mrs Cannon and of course nothing of the mystery of the tape connected with the answerphone. Other reporters came later and once or twice she was questioned on the telephone, but the police, that was say, Detective-Constable Miller, did not appear until about half past six.

He came in looking shy and sheepish, as if he felt he had no right to trouble her at all, then told her that he was sure that she had had a trying day.

'One or two things have come up,' he said as they both sat down, 'and perhaps you can tell me something about them. But we haven't got far. Nowhere at all really, but of course it's early days. All the same, we've one or two witnesses and that's more than you can usually expect. Surprising, you might say.'

He spoke jerkily as if it took a considerable mental effort to put words together at all.

'Witnesses?' Sara said incredulously. 'To the General's murder?'

'No, not exactly that,' he answered. 'To a caller at the house. You remember how it was raining?'

'Yes, of course.'

'Well, someone who was going up the High Street about ten o'clock, a young fellow who'd been stood up by his girlfriend and had tried to while the time away while he was waiting for her by having a few drinks and so wasn't in the best of tempers about things in general and not the best of witnesses, you might say, swears he saw a door which he's sure was General Schofield's open and an old man let somebody into the house, then shut the door. And all he can tell us about his visitor is that he thinks it was a man and that he was wearing an anorak with the hood up over his head. Can't describe him, can't say if he was tall or short, only feels fairly sure that he was very wet. But he could hardly help being that, could he?'

'In other words, this witness of yours didn't really tell you anything at all, except that General Schofield probably admitted a visitor at about ten o'clock,' Sara said, 'and you aren't sure you can rely on him for that.'

The constable gave a pleased smile, as if it reassured him to find that he had made himself so clear.

'Exactly,' he said. 'But there's our other witness. A man driving past in his car after having had dinner at the Red Lion. Had also had had a few drinks, he admits, but nothing to speak of. Says he thinks the time was about ten o'clock. And he saw a door open that he thinks was General Schofield's and an old man let somebody in. And he thinks it was a man, but of course he only had a back view of him so it might have been a tall woman, but whoever it was was wearing an anorak with the hood up and looked pretty wet.'

'It does all sound rather vague,' Sara said. 'I suppose you've spent today hunting for a wet anorak.'

'Exactly,' Miller said again. 'Not necessarily wet, that's to say. It could have had time to dry out overnight. But an anorak of any kind, and if by chance it turned out that there was some blood on it . . . It's likely, you know, that the murderer got some blood on himself which he may not have been aware of. Someone tall in an anorak, that's what we're looking for.'

'And have I got an anorak, isn't that what you want to know?' Sara said.

She believed that the constable blushed slightly. It astonished her that a policeman could blush.

'I was going to come to that presently,' he admitted. 'But although you're a fairly tall lady, I wouldn't have thought you could be mistaken for a man, even in an anorak. But if you wouldn't mind telling me . . .' He waited hopefully.

'I haven't,' she said. 'I've an ordinary raincoat. But if you'd like to, you can hunt through the flat. It won't take long. I brought very few things with me.'

'What I really wanted to ask,' he said, 'is whether you've seen anyone else in an anorak. I know it isn't likely in the hot sort of weather we've been having unless they were actually out in the rain yesterday evening, but it's a question we're asking everyone. They're kind of concealing garments, wouldn't you say, especially with a hood up? But if it just happened that you should have caught sight of anyone . . .' Again he waited.

Sara shook her head. 'No,' she said.

But of course she had seen Paul Fryer in an anorak the evening before and perhaps because of that sometimes awkward habit of truthfulness that she had, telling a direct lie made her fell self-conscious and she followed it up by humming a little tune. It was the tune of 'The Derby Ram', of all unfortunate things, for the words of it, though she did not sing them aloud, were:

> '"And indeed, sir, it's true, sir,
> I never was given to lie . . ."'

And Detective-Constable Miller recognized the tune and sang the remaining lines of the verse just audibly:

> '"And if you'd been to Derby, sir,
> You'd have seen it as well as I."'

At that point Sara began to have a higher regard for his mentality than she had had until then.

'Is that one of the songs you learnt at school and have never been able to forget?' she asked.

'That's right,' he said. 'And if I'd heard it only yesterday, I'd have forgotten it by now. Maybe it's the same with you.'

'Yes, it is,' she said.

'You learnt it at school?'

'Yes, we learnt a lot of old folk songs.'

'And did they teach you the last verse, I wonder.'

'I'm not sure. It's the refrain I really remember.'

'Well, the last verse isn't very nice. Perhaps they didn't think it was right to teach it to young kids:

> "The man that killed the ram, sir,
> "Was up to his knees in blood.
> "And the boy that held the pail, sir,
> "Was carried away in the flood."'

'All right, Constable,' she said, 'Mr Fryer has an anorak, but I'm sure you know that already. You just wanted to see if I was going to lie about it.'

'Well, yes, Mrs Marriott, as a matter of fact we did know that, and it's been taken into the lab to see if there are any bloodstains on it. I suppose you've never been to Derby.'

'No. Have you?'

'No. I was just wondering how Derby people seem to have got their reputation for exaggerating things a bit.'

'I don't know. But I'm sure there won't be any stains on Mr Fryer's anorak. He couldn't have any possible reason to harm General Schofield.'

'I don't think we've far to look for the motive for his murder,' Miller said. 'He knew, or someone thought he knew, something about the death of Mrs Cannon. And that's why we've been at the Agricultural College, asking questions about that missing tape of yours. It could have something to do with her death, we can't help thinking. But we didn't get far. And apart from that, you know, we've no evidence at all about her death.'

'It was suggested to me today that that tape never existed,' Sara said. 'What do you think about that?'

'We've considered that possibility, naturally,' he said.

'And how did it strike you when you'd considered it?'

'Well, that we can't see any point in your making up a yarn like that.' He gave a little shake of his head. 'We can't see any point in it at all.'

'Suppose I'm one of those people who likes drawing attention to herself by making things up. There are plenty of people like that, aren't there?'

'Oh yes, the people who write in or ring up confessing to crimes they've never committed and all that. But somehow the story of your tape doesn't seem to fall into that category.'

'So what do you think about it?'

'As I said, we haven't got far. But it could be that someone, Miss Eldridge for instance, was trying to fake an alibi for someone, or just possibly was trying to make trouble for someone by trying to make it look as if that was what she was doing. And that would have to be Mr Kimberley, to go by all we've heard about her relationship with him.'

So the police had got as far as Paul Fryer had, or possibly farther.

'I don't understand about her trying to make trouble for someone,' Sara said.

'Well, if you're given an obviously fake alibi when you don't happen to need one, it could look suspicious, couldn't it?'

'That's getting awfully subtle.'

He fidgeted a little. 'That's what the Inspector said when I suggested it.'

'So it was your idea.'

'As a matter of fact, it was. And the Inspector didn't think anything of it. I don't really think much of it myself. I suppose it would have to mean that it was an alibi for herself she was trying to set up, and that would mean she had something to do with Mrs Cannon's death, but I can't

think why she should have wanted to prevent the Kimberleys getting Mrs Cannon's money, unless it was sheer
revenge on Mr Kimberley for not going off with her. No,
forget it. But you haven't seen anyone but Mr Fryer in an
anorak, you're sure of that?'

'Absolutely sure.'

'There's something else we're investigating at the
moment, but you won't be able to help us with that,' he
said. 'There were some muddy footprints in the house, some
of which were the General's own, but some that didn't fit
with his, though they look the same sort of mud. Some of
it's been sent off to the lab, of course, and they may be able
to tell us where it came from. That's all, I think, for the
moment, Mrs Marriott. Thank you for your help.'

Looking as diffidently apologetic as ever, he allowed Sara
to show him out of the flat.

When he had gone she thought of going down to Paul
Fryer's flat to see if he still wanted to go out with her to
Pietro's, but a number of thoughts were confusing her and
instead of leaving straight away she poured herself out some
sherry and tried to sort out what it was that was troubling
her. That Kay Eldridge might have wanted revenge on Ron
Kimberley for refusing to leave his wife and family for her
seemed not impossible, but if so, and she had set about it
in the way that Detective-Constable Miller had suggested,
she had certainly chosen a very complicated method. Sara
was not sure that she understood what he had been suggesting about Kay's purpose with the tape. As he had said,
it would be best to forget it. He had just been floundering
around, trying to sort out the puzzle. Yet she had a feeling
that he might not remain a constable for so very much
longer and that if she were to meet him again in another
year or so she might find herself having to call him sergeant.

But the odd thing was that the thing about which he had
assumed she would not be able to help him, the muddy

footprints in the General's house, was something about which Sara had what she thought might be a useful idea. The question was, would it turn out that the mud came from the Kimberleys' farm? For in the afternoon, when she and the General had been there together, the soil had been dry and dusty and she herself had found when she got home that her shoes had a thin coating of mud on them, which must have come from the dust that she had picked up at the farm being turned to mud during the short run that she had had to make through the pouring rain from the garage to the front door of the house.

That there were no muddy footprints on her own floor was due to the fact that she had had to climb two flights of stairs before she reached her flat, shedding the mud on the way. Besides that, she remembered that she had rubbed her shoes well on the doormat just inside the front door before she started up the stairs. But the General, who would also have had dust from the farm on his shoes, had had no stairs to climb but had walked straight into his house from the car across the wet pavement and so had almost certainly left muddy footprints on his carpets.

But if there were other footprints there with mud which turned out to match the mud on his shoes, even though they could not have been made by them, did not that mean that someone from the farm, almost certainly Ron Kimberley, had been in the house that evening?

Everything pointed to Ron Kimberley.

But was he a madman who would kill without a motive?

She did not believe it. Gulping her sherry, she went downstairs to Paul's basement flat.

They went to Pietro's and ordered dinner. They did not talk much about the murder, indeed they did not talk much at all. It felt peaceful to be quiet. Sara remembered that there had been occasions during her marriage when she and Mark had hardly spoken to one another for days on end, when they had gone out together for a meal and had not spoken, had even been careful not to meet each other's eyes, and there had been nothing peaceful about the silence of those times. There had been bitterness and resentment. But this evening the mood between her and Paul was something quite different and it seemed that they shared it without having to speak of it, or making excuses to one another for it. They spoke a little about Paul's decision to try to live on his writing, and about when Sara was likely to return to London and the possibility that when she did she might be occupied helping an old lady of ninety-one, who wrote children's stories, to write her memoirs. But it was not until they were drinking their coffee that Sara felt impelled to speak of the events of the day.

'Paul, I did something today I'm ashamed of,' she said. 'I told that man Miller that you'd an anorak.'

He smiled. 'Well, I have,' he said. 'You've seen it.'

'But I began by saying that I didn't know anyone who'd got one,' she said, 'and I ought to have stuck to that. But somehow he got it out of me. I think he's a rather clever man. He knew I was lying and truly I'm ashamed.'

'It's generally thought to be a bad thing to tell lies, or so I've always heard,' he said. 'But it isn't of that that you're ashamed, I gather.'

'No, it's just that I think that if you decide to tell a lie you ought to be able to stick to it. It's weak and stupid to let yourself be shown up almost at once. Anyway, I'm very sorry.'

'It doesn't matter at all,' he assured her. 'I think by the time he got round to you he'd already asked me about my anorak and taken it away with him. They're welcome to it. They won't find any bloodstains on it. Incidentally, he also took away a pair of my shoes. I don't think they'll tell them much either.'

'Miller came up with an odd idea,' Sara said. 'It was

that Kay might have poisoned Mrs Cannon to prevent Ron Kimberley inheriting her money. Revenge, because he wouldn't leave his wife and family for her. And he thought that my answerphone mystery might be part of a sort of fake alibi for him that was bound to be thought fishy and would get him into trouble. But he told me that Inspector Dalling thought that was altogether too subtle.'

'I'm inclined to say the same,' Paul said.

'I suppose so . . .' She frowned a little as she said it.

'You think there might be something in the idea?' he asked.

'Not really. And yet there's something about it that somehow worries me. It does at least suggest a motive of sorts.'

'There's someone whose motive stares one in the face,' Paul said, 'yet we've hardly talked about him.'

'Oliver, you mean.'

'Yes. And perhaps one should add Celia, though I doubt if she could have killed the General. But they might have been acting together. In fact, if either of them was in it, they probably were. But tell me something, Sara. When the General wanted you to drive him out to the Kimberley farm, did he tell you why?'

'He said he didn't really feel safe driving any more because of his eyesight.'

'I don't mean that. I mean, why did he want to visit the Kimberleys?'

'I don't think he actually said. I just took for granted he wanted a sort of family get-together because of the tragedy. But perhaps he had another reason . . .'

'Yes?'

She finished her coffee. 'I was just thinking of something that Oliver said to me this morning. He said there's a window in the men's room at the Red Lion from which you can see the Cannons' house, and he wondered if the General had seen someone either come to the house or leave it about two o'clock. But with his poor eyesight he might not have been sure who it was, yet he might have thought that it looked like Ron. And when we were out at the farm he wanted to know where Ron had been that afternoon, and he seemed to accept that he'd been at the farm and able to answer a telephone call from Kay, which gave him an alibi, so that he couldn't have been the person whom perhaps the General saw. So it might have been to make sure of that that we went to the farm. But then there's the call he made to me in the evening, saying he'd an idea about my answerphone problem which he'd tell me about this morning. Is that what you wanted to know?'

He nodded. 'More or less.'

'Anyway, let's be going home now. I'm really too tired to think reasonably about anything.'

'Me too.'

He paid the bill and the two of them strolled back through the warm summer evening to the Cannons' house.

They said goodbye to one another at the door and Sara wearily climbed the stairs to her flat. As she put the key in her door, which she had remembered to lock, she heard the telephone inside ringing. Because she was impatient to get to it, she fumbled clumsily with the key and was sure that the caller would have rung off before she could answer and that the call itself was certain to be something very important. But it was still ringing when she reached it, without having troubled to close the door behind her.

'Sara Marriott here,' she said.

'Mrs Marriott?' said a voice that sounded eerily familiar. 'This is Kay Eldridge. May I see you tomorrow morning? I could call in about nine o'clock, if that would suit you. There's something important I want to say to you.'

CHAPTER 9

So Kay's telephone was working now. But Sara was never to know what it was that she had intended to tell her. The body of a young woman, later to be identified as that of Kay Eldridge, was found among the reeds that bordered the slow-moving stream that crossed the Heath. Some children, throwing a ball for their dog to chase, had tossed it by mistake into the water and the dog, going plunging in after it, had disturbed a foot, a leg, then the rest of what had once been a human being, from its hiding-place among the tall reeds. But that did not happen until the afternoon. No one, until then, had been particularly looking for Kay. That she was missing had worried Sara, who had been expecting her, though she had been irritated rather than alarmed when she did not appear.

Sara had taken the trouble to get up a little earlier than usual, so that she should not only have had time to get dressed but to have had breakfast by the time that Kay was to have arrived. She had made more coffee than she needed for herself, so that she could offer some to Kay when she came, but nine o'clock passed and there was no ring at the doorbell. It was half past nine before Sara began to wonder if Kay had changed her mind and did not intend to come after all. At ten o'clock Sara opened the telephone directory to see if she could find Kay's number there, found it, with Kay's address, and tried dialling it, but received no answer. At that point she nearly gave up the attempt to make contact with her and thought that she would go out shopping to buy in some supplies that she needed from the supermarket if she was going to be staying on even for a short time longer in Edgewater. But then she thought that she might try telephoning the Agricultural College, found its number in the directory and on being answered when she dialled, asked if she could speak to Miss Eldridge.

After a slight delay she was answered by a voice that she did not recognize.

'This is Dr Canfield's secretary. Can I help you?'

'I wanted to speak to Miss Eldridge,' Sara replied. 'Is she in the College this morning?'

'Who is it speaking?' the voice asked.

'My name's Sara Marriott,' Sara replied. 'I was expecting to see Miss Eldridge this morning. She telephoned yesterday evening that she wanted to see me.'

'Well, I'm afraid she hasn't come in yet.' There was a slight pause. 'My name's Beatrice James. Kay and I share an office. She didn't come in yesterday either, but that was because she had a migraine. When she didn't show up this morning I tried ringing her up to ask her how she was, but didn't get any answer—I know her phone's been out of order—so I'm afraid I can't help you. Can I give her a message if she does come in presently?'

'Perhaps you'd just tell her that I rang,' Sara said.

'And you said your name is . . . ?'

'Sara Marriott. I gathered that there was something important that she wanted to say to me.'

'Are you connected with the police?'

'No.'

'It's just that they were here yesterday, asking questions about her, and so was someone else, I'm not sure who it was, all to do with that dreadful murder of the poor General, but of course I couldn't tell them anything much. But I'll give her your message, though I don't know if she'll come in at all. Actually it isn't like her to be unpunctual. She's usually here on the dot, or if something's happened like that headache yesterday she rings me up and lets me know about it.'

'Thank you,' Sara said.

'You're welcome.'

They both rang off. Sara sat where she was for a little while, looking thoughtfully at the telephone as if it could advise her what she ought to do. The unidentified caller on Beatrice James who had come asking questions the day before had certainly been Paul Fryer. But now a little worry about Kay's absence began to creep into Sara's mind. She spent another ten minutes or so deciding what to do next, then set off, walking briskly, towards the Heath and Kay's bungalow on the far side of it.

It was a very small bungalow in a row of others equally small, built close together except for the narrow car-ports between them, and all of a rather dreary red brick, without front gardens but only a long strip of gravel from which a few steps led up to their front doors. Sara went up to Kay's door and rang the bell. There was no answer. She rang it again and waited, but there was still no answer. After remaining where she was for a minute or two, she decided to see if by any chance Kay was in the garden at the back of the house, and set off along the narrow path that ran round it. Passing the car-port, she saw that a car, a bright red Mini, was inside it. But there was no one in the garden. It consisted only of a small square lawn enclosed by a wooden fence, with a few shrubs at the end of it and with a little patio on which a couple of garden chairs had been left out and on to which a glass door from a room at the back of the house opened. And this door was open.

Sara went to it, pushed it further open and called, 'Kay!'

There was only silence.

She tried calling louder and met only with the same silence. Hesitating once more, but with uneasiness, a feeling of something being mysteriously wrong, growing in her mind, she pushed the door open and stepped inside.

The room was a living-room that ran from the back to the front of the bungalow. From where she stood she could see through the window at the further end of the room out to the road. It was a gaudy little room with a carpet of yellowish green, green and white striped curtains, chairs covered in cream-coloured plastic and a dining table and chairs of pale imitation oak with legs of chrome. There were newspapers and women's magazines scattered on a couch. Seeing them made Sara suddenly think of something to which she had paid no attention when she had first arrived at the house. There had been a newspaper pushed half way in at the letter-box. Also there had been a milk bottle on the doorstep.

She tried to think what a milk bottle might mean. Probably it meant that Kay's milkman did not come round very early in the morning and that Kay had set out to wherever she had gone before his arrival. But it could mean something somewhat more sinister. The sense of something sinister in the little house was growing in Sara and suddenly she made up her mind to see if there was any justification for this. Calling out, 'Kay!' several times and still receiving no answer, she set off to explore the rest of the bungalow.

She found a bedroom in which the bed had either been made early or had not been slept in, a miniature bathroom and a kitchen which was very neat and clean. There were no unwashed dishes in the sink, no food left out of the fridge or the canisters in which it belonged. Kay, it was evident, was a very careful housewife. Sara made her way back to the living-room and was about to leave it by the door into the garden when her eyes fell on the telephone and a sudden thought made her pause. Kay had once burgled Sara's flat and stolen a tape. So why, now that Sara had entered Kay's home, also uninvited, should she not see if she could find the tape in it?

The search that she made was necessarily superficial and she found nothing. But that could have meant simply that the tape was well hidden. Alternatively, it could have meant that it had been destroyed. Whichever might be the case, an attempt to find it simply by opening a few drawers and cupboards was futile. She did not persist for long and, returning from the kitchen to the living-room to let herself out into the garden, came face to face with Celia Hancock.

Celia was in her usual shirt and slacks which from a distance might have made it difficult to be sure if she were a man or a woman, if it had not been for the pony-tail of brown hair tied back from her face. It looked pale and tired this morning, with smudges of shadow under her wide-spaced brown eyes. But when she saw Sara they brightened with a look of anger.

'What are you doing here?' she demanded as she stepped into the room.

'Looking for Kay,' Sara answered. 'She rang me up yesterday, saying she wanted to see me.'

'And isn't she here?'

'No.'

'Then how did you get in?'

'The same way as you did. The door was open.'

'But was she expecting you?'

'I can't really say she was,' Sara replied, 'I was expecting her. When she rang me up yesterday evening, she said she'd call in on me this morning because there was something important she wanted to say to me, but she didn't come. So I tried phoning her and got no answer and I tried phoning the College, but was told she hadn't come in, so I had the idea that I'd come to look for her here.'

'And this door was open?'

'Yes.'

Celia dropped into a chair and, leaning back for a

moment, covered her eyes. It looked unlikely that she had
slept the night before. Then with a sigh she sat up and slid
a hand over her hair as if she was pushing it back from her
face, although it was perfectly smooth.

'It isn't like her,' she said in a tired voice. 'She's usually
very punctual and very efficient. You know she's Oliver's
secretary, don't you? He says she's the best he's ever had.
How long have you been waiting for her?'

'She said she'd call on me in my flat about nine o'clock.'

'No, I meant in here.'

'I'm not sure. About twenty minutes or so, I suppose.
Was she expecting you?'

'No, I only made up my mind to come a few minutes
ago. I walked along from the College. I wanted to see if I
could get the truth out of her about that answerphone tape
of yours.'

'So you do believe it exists?'

Celia gave Sara a long look, seeming to be debating with
herself how to answer. At last she said, 'I think I ought to
apologize to you for what I said about that yesterday. I'd
no right whatever to say what I did.'

'Then you do believe it exists,' Sara insisted.

A little frown appeared on Celia's forehead. 'Whether or
not it does, I'd no right to call you a liar, which is what I
did,' she said. 'And I do apologize. And I thought that
if I could get the truth about it out of Kay, I mean
if she'd admit that she had it and perhaps might even
show it to me, then I'd try to persuade her at least to
tell the police about it. Isn't that what you wanted to do
yourself?'

Sara had sat down in another of the cream-coloured
chairs.

'I'm not sure. She said she had something important to
say to me, but it didn't necessarily have to be about the
tape. She knew that I'd been out to the Kimberley farm

with General Schofield yesterday afternoon and she might have had something to say about that. But I suppose you're right, I wanted to sort out the business about the tape.'

'Do you know that General Schofield left all his money divided equally between the Kimberley twins?' Celia asked.

'No,' Sara said. 'I haven't heard anything about that.'

'Oliver heard it yesterday from the General's solicitor, who was also Mrs Cannon's. And of course Meg and Ron know about it too by now,' Celia said. 'There isn't a great deal. He'd been living mostly on his pension, with a small amount of capital inherited from his father, which once would have seemed a quite generous amount, but isn't worth much now. It's been left in trust, of course, and is just about enough to cover the twins' education at Granborough. Not that that's how it's actually got to be spent. If Ron and Meg sell the farm and move away they might have other ideas, but it has to be spent for the children's benefit, or else kept till they're of age. Did you know that Ron and Meg were thinking of moving?'

'I did, as a matter of fact. Meg told the General about it when we were out at the farm.'

'Oliver and I have known about it for some time. They'd have got a good deal more money out of the job Ron was offered in Reading than they ever made from the farm and it was particularly the cost of the children's education that was worrying them. But now that that's taken care of, I don't know whether they'll go. I rather wish they would. I don't think Ron's really a very dedicated farmer and I don't think Meg's ever liked the place much. If she'd had any money of her own I think she'd probably have left him.'

'But if she'd divorced him, which she easily could have done over his awfully public affair with Kay, wouldn't he have had to pay Meg maintenance?'

'Yes, but it wouldn't have been much, as he hadn't much himself.'

'Not enough for her to live on and go on with her sculpture?'

'Perhaps. Of course, if Mrs Cannon hadn't died just when she did—' Celia stopped and looked as if she wished that she had not spoken.

'Celia, do you really believe Ron killed Mrs Cannon?' Sara asked.

Celia did not answer. She stared straight in front of her, but it was as if what she was seeing was a long way away.

'You've been doing some thinking, I believe,' Sara went on. 'At first you thought the best thing would be to convince the police that the tape had never existed and that I was just trying to make trouble for you all by pretending that it had. Then you realized that if it could be found and shown to them, and the message on it hadn't simply been erased, it would go a long way to destroying Ron's alibi, because if he claimed he'd had a telephone call at the farm when in fact the call had been made to my answerphone and he need not have been at the farm at all to answer it, the alibi that that call was intended to give him would be blown to bits. And so you came here to see if you could find the tape, and perhaps frighten Kay somehow into giving it to you. Only what puzzles me is why you should think it's necessary, unless it's to protect Oliver. But you yourself have given Oliver an alibi. You said you were having lunch with him in the College canteen at the time when the drug must have been put into Mrs Cannon's coffee. So unless that isn't true, or at least not entirely true, because it's possible, I suppose, that you didn't spend very long together and he could have gone home after you separated, why should you worry about whether the tape existed?'

Celia suddenly sprang to her feet, her eyes blazing as they now met Sara's directly.

'And what business is it of yours if there's anything wrong with Oliver's alibi, or Ron's alibi, or even mine?' she cried in a voice that was almost a shout. 'You come here from God knows where to do a job of work for a poor old man who's been horribly killed, and that's the end of the job and how it all happened has nothing to do with you! So why don't you get out of the way? Why don't you go home? Nobody wants you here. If that tape existed, it wasn't intended for you. Don't keep creeping around, snooping and making crazy accusations against people you know nothing about. Get out! Go away!'

The suddenness of it almost startled Sara into losing her temper in return. The apparent self-control of naturally shy people can be very superficial and their own anger can be something that they fear more than the rage of others. The heat that shot through Sara as she too sprang up from her chair filled her for a moment with a kind of terror. Her face was very pale as she stood staring at Celia. Then she took refuge in one of the simplest of defences. She laughed.

'We're both making fools of ourselves,' she said. 'Of course I'd go home at once if I could, and I'm sure you know that. But the police haven't yet said I can go.'

'They can't keep you here unless they charge you with something.'

'But they can indicate that they'd like me to stay.'

Celia drew one or two deep breaths, her chest heaving. Then she walked towards the door into the garden.

'All right,' she said. 'I apologize. I apologize again. I seem to do nothing but apologize to you. Of course you're quite right that I'm frightened about Oliver, because we only spent about twenty minutes together in the canteen. Then I went off to my lab and I presume he went to his room. That's what he told me and I believe him. But there may have been people who saw us leave earlier than we told the police we did. We did that just to save trouble, not because we felt guilty, but it could look bad if they hear about it. So I thought I'd see if I could find anything wrong with Ron's alibi. But even if there is, I wish him luck. That mother of Oliver's was just a bloody old bitch, selfish to her fingertips, ready to make a mess of anyone's life if it suited her convenience. She's no loss to anyone. Nobody cared for her.'

'Not even Oliver a little?'

Celia shrugged her shoulders. 'I suppose he did in a way, but it was more that he felt she was dependent on him than that he actually loved her. That's why I'd no conscience about trying to get him away from her.'

'Will you be going to Canada now?'

'I expect so. But I don't know how long we'll have to stay here or how long the offer there will stay open. In any case, it doesn't much matter what we do now, does it? Oliver's free and we've plenty of money—the money you probably think he killed the old woman to get. And I'm not going to apologize for saying that's what you probably think, because I'm sure it's true. Goodbye.'

She walked away quickly into the garden and out of sight.

Sara waited for about five minutes after she had gone, then also went out by the way that she had come in. She walked back across the Heath, staying near to the stream without guessing how close she came to the sinister thing that lay hidden in the reeds. For a little while she sat on a bench, gazing away at the green slopes of the Downs, though at first hardly seeing them. She was wondering how soon she would actually be able to go home, thinking at first that she would like to go that very day, but then thinking that perhaps she did not really want to go until she had at least seen Paul once more. She would like to be up on those Downs with him now, talking of whatever had nothing to do with murder. But how absurd. Why should she want to do that? How little she really knew herself. Or Paul either, for that matter.

Getting up after a while, she walked back to the Cannons' house and was about to go in at the door when something stopped her. Chained to the railing above the entrance to Paul's basement flat were two bicycles, and standing in the area at his doorway, waiting to be let in, were the Kimberley twins.

Paul looked up and saw Sara at the top of the steps.

'How about coming in for a drink?' he asked. Then he turned to the twins. 'And what's brought you?'

'Please, we'd like to come in for a talk,' Jill said.

Sara descended the steps. She followed the twins into Paul's living-room. It looked as if he had been interrupted at his work, for there was a sheet of paper in the typewriter on his table with only a few lines written on it. The twins, in their usual jeans and T-shirts, went forward with more appearance of shyness than was usual with them to the middle of the room, then stood still, looking diffidently round them.

'Sherry?' Paul said to Sara, and when she said, 'Please,' went on to say to the twins, 'I've no Coca-Cola, I'm afraid, but I could manage some orange juice.'

'Thank you,' they both murmured politely and Paul disappeared into his kitchen to fetch the drinks.

While he was gone, Jill said, 'We aren't sure if we ought to have come. It was just an idea we had.'

'But we had to do something,' Nick said. 'It's been getting so that we couldn't stand things.'

'Only we aren't sure if we ought to have come to Paul or to Oliver,' Jill went on, 'but it's really much easier to talk to Paul.'

'And Oliver might be at work, and Celia too,' Nick said.

'And anyway, he may be mixed up in things more than Paul, because he's family—' Jill broke off as Paul reappeared, carrying a tray with two glasses filled with orange juice and two others with sherry. 'Are we being an awful nuisance, Paul?' she asked.

He handed out the glasses.

'I shan't be able to tell you that till you tell me why you've come,' he answered. 'But I generally consider it a pleasure to see you. Are you hungry?'

'Yes, but don't bother about it,' she said. 'We can do something about that later. We've got some money.'

'I'm afraid I can't give you an honest to goodness lunch,' he said, 'but I could manage some ham sandwiches presently, if you can survive on that.' He turned to Sara. 'Will you join us in some ham sandwiches?'

'Thank you, unless we all go out to the Green Tree Café,' she said. 'What about that?'

'Well, what about it?' Paul asked the twins. 'Come as my guests.'

They exchanged glances, both looking torn between the sandwiches that they had been offered and the fine fare that they imagined they might be given at the café. But either politeness, because the sandwiches had been offered first and it was their friend Paul who had offered them, or else some other feeling that they shared, won, and they said that please, they would sooner stay where they were.

'It's all so difficult to explain,' Jill said, 'but we had to do something.'

She sat down on the floor, cross-legged, nursing her orange juice, while Nick found a corner of a sofa that was free of books and papers and sat down there, drawing his legs up under him. Sara sat down on the upright chair at the table where the typewriter was and sipped her sherry, watching the children with a good deal of curiosity because it seemed to her that whatever had brought them was something of desperate seriousness to them. Paul remained standing on the hearth-rug in front of the unlit fire.

'Well?' he said.

'It's all that quarrelling,' Jill said. 'They're at it all the time now and we can't stand it.'

'Ron and Meg, do you mean?' Paul asked.

Both the children nodded.

'What do they quarrel about?'

'Us,' Jill said.

'I don't think I understand,' Paul said. 'About how you're being brought up, or what you'll do when you're older, or your staying at Granborough, or something like that?'

'No, no, just us,' she said. 'About which of them we love most and that sort of thing. It's very embarrassing.'

'Because of course we love them both about the same,' Nick said. 'I mean, that's only natural, isn't it?'

Sara could think of several people whom she had known who had certainly very much preferred one parent to the other, not always choosing wisely, but if the twins thought such a state of affairs unnatural she did not want to disturb their faith.

'But do they do this in front of you?' she asked.

'Not exactly, but we can hear them,' Jill said. 'As a matter of fact . . .' She hesitated.

'As a matter of fact, when we think they're at it,' Nick said, 'we go and listen at the door, and when we're sure that's what they're doing we get on our bikes and ride away. But today somehow we got the feeling that we couldn't face going back, because when we do, after one of those rows, they're both ever so nice to us, almost as if they mean— well, I don't really know how to say it.'

'Mean to compete for your affections,' Paul suggested.
Both twins nodded eagerly.

'That's just it,' Jill said, 'only it's so difficult to put it
into words. So we thought we'd like to talk to someone else
about it and we thought you'd be the best person. Because,
you see, we've got money now, haven't we? General
Schofield left us his money, did you know that? And so we
ought to be able to make up our minds for ourselves what
to do, we haven't just got to go on putting up with things.
But we thought we'd like to discuss it with someone who'd
be able to advise us.'

Paul thrust his fingers through his hair in a gesture of
some desperation.

'Oh my God, you don't know what you're asking!'
he exclaimed. 'My dears, you can't do anything like
that.'

'Why not?' Jill asked. 'It's our money, isn't it?'

'But what you mean is, you're thinking of leaving home
and living on this money of yours, and you want me to tell
you how to set about it.'

'We did wonder if we could actually stay with you,' Nick
said. 'Only during these holidays, of course, because when
the term starts we'd go to Granborough, but if we could
stay with you here, we'd pay you for everything and we'd
be ever so careful not to be any trouble. But if you don't
like the idea, perhaps you could tell us where we might
go.'

'I need another drink,' Paul said abruptly. 'What about
you, Sara?'

'Not yet, thank you,' she answered.

He disappeared once more into the kitchen to fetch one
for himself.

Jill looked at Sara. 'He isn't angry with us, is he?' she
asked anxiously. 'I mean, it was only an idea.'

'I don't think he's in the least angry,' Sara said. 'It's just that you've set him a rather peculiar problem. He's going to have to explain something to you.'

After a moment Paul returned. He took up his place again on the hearth-rug.

'Now listen to me, you two,' he said, 'because I've got to get you to understand some things. First of all, you haven't any money at all just at present. It can be spent on your education, or otherwise for your benefit, by your trustee, whoever he is, but you won't be able to touch it yourselves till you're of age, and that's a long way off. And very welcome as you'd be to stay with me here, you can't simply run out on your parents without letting them know where you are or what you're up to. For all we know, they may already be sick with worry about your disappearance and be thinking of phoning all the local hospitals or even the police.'

'Oh no, they won't be doing that,' Nick said. 'We often go off for the day without telling them much about where we're going.'

'All the same, as soon as I've had this drink, I'm going to phone them,' Paul said.

'Are you afraid they might think you'd kidnapped us?' Jill said. 'If they found us, we'd tell them it was all our own idea. They've often lectured us, you know, about not speaking to strange men, but you're not exactly a strange man, are you, Paul?'

'I'm feeling very strange at the moment,' he answered. 'I've never been asked to help abduct anyone before. Now what's your phone number?'

Suddenly and violently Jill burst into tears.

'But we can't go back!' she stormed. 'Those awful quarrels! And they aren't our fault, really they aren't our fault! You may think they are, but we've never done anything to make them happen! We're always just the same to both of them.'

Paul finished his sherry, gave a deep sigh and said, 'All right, we'll have our sandwiches first and talk a bit about it all afterwards, and then I'll phone them. D'you like mustard with your ham?'

'Yes, please,' Jill said, while Nick said, 'No, thank you,' and Sara also refused it and Paul disappeared once more into the kitchen.

They were all quiet and rather subdued over their sandwiches, then Paul offered to make coffee but the twins chose more orange juice. He made coffee for Sara and himself, then when they were all supplied with what they had chosen he began again to explain to the twins that the money that they believed was theirs was not actually available to them yet, and also that he thought it was time for him to let their parents know where they were. They listened this time without making any protest and once he was sure that they understood their position, he asked them again for the telephone number of the farm and dialled it.

When someone answered, he said, 'Meg? This is Paul. In case you're wondering what's happened to your offspring, I've got them here . . . What? . . . Oh, having lunch of a sort . . . I don't understand, Meg. Of course, if that's what you want, for as long as you like, but what's the matter? . . . *What?* . . . Oh, I see . . . Well, ring me back as soon as you can . . . No! . . . I still don't understand, but don't worry about the kids, at least they're all right. Goodbye.'

It would have reminded Sara of the one-sided conversation to which she had listened on her answerphone if she had not been able to hear a voice that sounded high and excitable, even though she could not distinguish any of the words, speaking to Paul from the other end of the line. As he put the telephone down he stood still for a moment, looking straight before him with a shocked frown on his forehead, then still looking as if he were thinking of something else, he started collecting the plates and cups and glasses that had been used for lunch and, without speaking, carried them out to the kitchen.

After a moment Sara followed him, murmuring something to the children about helping him to wash up, and found him standing at the sink where he had stacked the crockery, with one hand on a tap as if he were about to turn it on, but in fact only staring before him still, doing nothing.

Sara dropped her voice to a whisper in case what she said could be heard by the twins in the living-room.

'What's the matter, Paul?'

He turned his head to look at her, but still with the same unseeing expression in his eyes.

'They're taking Ron to the police station to "help them in their inquiries",' he answered in a tone as soft as the one in which she had spoken. 'And Meg wants me to keep the kids here for the present, to keep them out of the way. It sounds as if they've absolutely clear evidence against him for Schofield's murder. They found an anorak at the farm that's got blood on one cuff, and a pair of Ron's shoes that match the prints on the General's carpets, and there's more than one witness who saw Ron's car parked in the market square around ten o'clock that night. And there's something about a telephone call that I didn't understand. Meg was too distraught to make much sense, but it sounds as if the General phoned Ron that evening, she doesn't know about what, but as soon as he'd done it Ron got the car out and drove off.' Talking seemed to have relieved the extreme tension that he had felt after his conversation with Meg and he began to rinse the cups and saucers under the tap. 'It looks an open-and-shut case, doesn't it?'

'Oh, the poor children!' Sara said. 'Let me know if I can help you with them. But what's Ron's motive supposed to have been? Had the General some evidence that Ron had killed Mrs Cannon?'

'Meg didn't say anything about that,' Paul replied. 'She did say something about "the money", but I couldn't follow it.'

'Perhaps the money Ron knew the General was leaving the children,' Sara suggested. 'It won't take the place of what Mrs Cannon would have left them, but I suppose it would help. Only I can't believe that somehow.'

'In any case, Ron must have been half out of his mind to be so careless,' Paul said. 'Leaving his car where anyone could see, it, leaving those footmarks, leaving the blood on his sleeve—' He broke off as the sound of the door-knocker penetrated to the kitchen.

He went to answer it and Sara followed him. As they passed through the living-room it looked to Sara as if the twins in themselves were not going to be much of a problem. Both of them had found books that appeared to attract them on Paul's bookshelves and were sitting on the floor with the books on their laps. Paul went to his door and opened it. Detective-Constable Miller stood there.

'Good afternoon,' he said in his usual diffident but courteous way. 'I happened to be passing . . . I mean, it happened that I wanted to go upstairs to see if Mr Cannon was in, but he seems to be out at work, and as I had this . . .' He held out something that he was holding which Sara recognized as Paul's dark blue anorak. 'Well, I thought I'd return it, and while I was at it—' But there he broke off suddenly, having just caught sight of the twins in the room behind Paul. A look of dismay appeared on his face. 'I didn't know you'd company,' he said.

Paul stepped out into the area and would have closed the door behind him if Sara had not slipped out after him. She was aware that both the children had lowered their books and were listening intently.

'Something you don't want them to hear?' she asked as she drew the door shut after her.

'Well, yes, I wouldn't much like to be the one who has to tell them what's been happening,' the constable answered.

'You mean that you've arrested their father for murder?' Paul said.

'For both murders, though he hasn't been charged yet,' Miller answered. 'He's only been taken in for questioning.'

'*Both* murders?' Paul exclaimed, then gave a scowl because he had forgotten to keep his voice down. 'You mean you're probably going to charge him with Mrs Cannon's murder?'

The constable looked bewildered. 'Mrs Cannon's? I thought they were clear that was suicide. It was just one of the Inspector's fancy ideas that it might have been murder. No . . . Oh, you haven't heard.' He sounded surprised, but Sara felt sure that there was something that he knew perfectly well that they had not heard. 'No, the body of a Miss Eldridge, with whom I believe you were acquainted, was found this afternoon in the stream across the Heath. It had been there for some hours, we believe, and wasn't found sooner because it had got pushed into the reeds. She'd been strangled with the cord of her dressing-gown. And Mr Kimberley's car was seen near her bungalow late last night and a neighbour saw a man in an anorak carrying something that looked like a woman from that house towards the Heath. And there are his fingerprints in the house, though we understand they may have been there for some time, as he was a fairly frequent visitor, and may have no significance at the moment. What may mean more is that there don't seem to be anyone else's but his and hers. But I wouldn't like the kids to hear all this.'

'I'm not surprised.' Paul looked searchingly into the other man's face. 'And you aren't interested in Mrs Cannon's death any more?'

'I wouldn't exactly say that,' Miller replied. 'I mean, we've got to wait for the inquest. But there's really no evidence that it was murder, is there? A book on the floor and the question of how she got hold of the drug. That's not much to go on. There are all kinds of ways of getting hold of drugs these days, as you must know yourself, Mr Fryer. Now, I'm sorry to have disturbed you. You didn't see Miss Eldridge yourself yesterday, I suppose.'

Paul shook his head.

Sara said, 'But she rang me up yesterday evening and said she wanted to call in on me this morning about nine o'clock to tell me something important. But she never came and I don't know what she wanted to tell me.'

'Nine o'clock. Mm, yes, she'd have been dead some time by then,' Miller said. 'Would it have been something to do with that answerphone tape she wanted to tell you about, d'you think?'

'I think it's quite likely,' Sara replied.

'Pity it's vanished. Queer to talk like that to nobody. "But answer came there none, And that was scarcely odd because he'd murdered every one . . ." Sorry, that's a misquotation. I suppose it slipped out like that because I've got murder so much on my mind. This is the first case of murder I've ever been involved in. But d'you know, I believe I could repeat that poem from beginning to end even now, though I learnt it when I was about six or so. And I remember I took it all for granted, I mean that it was quite natural for a walrus and a carpenter to be the best of friends. Queer the things you'll take for granted when you're that age. And when you're a lot older, if it comes to that. You take for granted, for instance, that it's natural to murder to get hold of some money, but some people might think it was natural to do it to prevent yourself getting that money. After all, that's not impossible. The more I see in my job, the less impossible everything seems to be.'

'I wonder why you became a policeman,' Sara said. 'You aren't exactly my idea of one.'

'It's a job,' he said laconically. 'But I'm taking up your time. Sorry about the kids, they've a tough time coming.'

He thrust the anorak into Paul's arms and hurried up the steps to the street.

Paul and Sara stayed where they were for a moment, looking at one another. Then Paul said, 'He believes Mrs Cannon was murdered and that Ron did it, but he knows they're never going to be able to prove it.'

'Yet it's where everything began,' Sara said.

'Of course.' He put an arm round her. 'Now let's go in.'

CHAPTER 10

No one ever proved that Althea Cannon had been murdered. At the inquest into her death an open verdict was returned. How she obtained the drug that killed her was never explained, but it was thought not impossible that she had somehow done so herself, and the insignificant fact that there had been a book on the floor by her bed when her body was found was not even mentioned. She was cremated, her ashes were strewn over a rose-bed in the Garden of Remembrance, and her story was ended.

Ronald Allington Kimberley was found guilty of the murders of General Arthur Schofield and Kathleen Eldridge. He had left a trail behind him so broad that there was never any doubt what the verdict would be and he was sentenced to life imprisonment. That something might have happened to make him lose his sense of reality before embarking on his career of murder was thought not improbable, but the prosecution was not obliged to prove that this was so. His car had been seen close to the scene of each crime at each critical time, his footprints had been found on the General's carpets, blood that matched the General's had been found on the cuff of his anorak and he had actually been seen carrying the body of a woman from Kay Eldridge's bungalow to the bridge over the stream that crossed the Heath and bundling it into the water. That the two witnesses to this had not come forward earlier than they did was because they had had no wish to be found together.

The question of motive was discussed, but it was not necessary for the prosecution to prove it. It was supposed that he had been bitterly disappointed when he had been told that the money that he and his wife would inherit from Mrs Cannon was not in fact to be theirs, and that when General Schofield had telephoned him on the evening before his murder, possibly to tell him that he was providing for the children's education in his will, the temptation to kill him had been too strong to resist. Then that murder was followed by the murder of Ron's mistress because she knew too much about him and somehow he discovered that she had telephoned Sara Marriott, intending to tell her what she knew on the following morning. Why she should have chosen to tell this to Sara Marriott, whom she scarcely knew, was found puzzling but not very important. People did strange things. No questions relating to a tape on an answerphone were raised. Ron's behaviour at his trial was silent and sullen and Sara, who had to be there, felt that his mind had given way perhaps before she had ever even met him at that sad eightieth birthday party at the Cannons' house in Edgewater. But then there were things that she knew that were never discussed at the trial.

Long before it, in the afternoon when the twins were sitting contentedly reading in Paul Fryer's living-room, and Detective-Constable Miller had left and Sara and Paul had returned to the room she had felt inclined to believe that she more or less understood the truth about the death of Althea Cannon. But for the moment all that she could think about were the children. They were going to have to learn that their father was probably about to be arrested for murder. Someone was going to have to explain this to them. Not herself. Nor, she thought, Paul. It would have to be Meg who would have to face this fearful duty, but until she came to collect the children the only thing to be done was to avoid the subject. But this meant virtually avoiding talk of any kind, because it was impossible to think of anything else. Luckily the twins had found books that absorbed them, and Sara, following a lead given by Paul, chose a book from his bookshelf and settled down to pretend to read it. Except that there was a programme on the radio which the twins said they always listened to when they could and asked if they might have it on now, the afternoon passed away almost in silence.

Meg arrived about five o'clock to collect the children, or rather to tell them to get on to their bicycles and ride home. She stayed for only a few minutes and when Paul began to ask a tentative question about what had been happening at the farm, she only scowled at him and grasping each child by a shoulder, told them to hurry up.

'Another time,' she muttered to Paul, showing that she was not yet ready for there to be any discussion in front of the children of the calamity that had struck her family.

She had arrived by a hired car and had driven away in it, after she had made sure that the twins had set off homeward on their bicycles. The Kimberleys' own car had been impounded by the police. Once they had all gone the room seemed even more silent than it had been while they were there, and empty and desolate. Later Meg sold the farm and, to the surprise of most people who knew her, bought herself an old cottage in a village in the Highlands of Scotland. What she had made by selling the farm was just enough for her to live on. The children continued their education at Granborough, but spent their holidays very happily with their mother and at least for a time became fervent Scottish Nationalists. That it had been wise to take them away from Edgewater seemed to be proved, and at Granborough their situation was treated with a sensitivity that made Sara think more highly of her old school than she ever had before. Paul stuck to his decision of resigning from the staff and living by his pen, and after a time found a flat for himself in Battersea.

But in the evening after Meg and the twins had left the Cannons' house and after a drink or two, Paul and Sara went out for dinner at Pietro's. Once there, with their tinned jellified consomme and their omelettes and their house wine, it felt easier to talk than in the house that seemed haunted by the death of Mrs Cannon and by the presence of the children who had not known of the disaster that had already happened to them.

'They'll never prove anything,' Paul said, 'even if they're fairly sure what happened, but I think we can work it out for ourselves, don't you?'

Sara nodded absently. 'I suppose so. It began with Mrs Cannon deciding to change her will, didn't it, and leave all she had to the Kimberleys? Do you know, I believe I was with her when she was making up her mind to do that? I'd just arrived at the house to ask about the flat and I met Oliver coming out, looking as if he were in a fearful temper. And then Mrs Cannon found it very difficult to think about the flat at all, but told me she'd at last made up her mind about something she was going to do. And I think that was to change her will.'

'Yes, but she didn't mean to leave her money to the Kimberley family,' Paul said. 'She was going to leave it to Meg. We've all been thinking that that was the same as leaving it to the family, but of course it wasn't, not in a family like that, because what do you think Meg would have done if she'd suddenly inherited a lot of money?'

'You mean she'd have left Ron?'

'Don't you think she would? Or don't you think that Ron might at least have believed that she would?'

'And so he murdered Mrs Cannon to stop Meg doing that? But surely he didn't care for her as much as all that.'

'I think he cared very little for her. But he doted on those children. And he guessed that if Meg wasn't financially dependent on him any more, the first thing she'd do would be to divorce him, and with the Eldridge affair what it was there wouldn't have been much difficulty about that, and almost for certain she'd have got custody of the children. Of course he'd have had right of access to them at stated times, but she could have taken them away from him. And she would have, I'm quite sure. Though she never paraded her affection for them as he did, that didn't mean she felt any less.'

'So you think that was the motive we haven't been able to find. He didn't want Meg to be financially able to leave him, taking the children.'

'Well, don't you think so?'

She considered it, frowning a little, then nodded. 'Some people would have left him anyway and looked for a job, but I suppose she wanted him to go on paying for her sculpture. She said herself to the General and me that it was an expensive occupation. It's especially expensive if you want to work in bronze, she said. Well, and so Ron decided to kill his aunt before she'd time to change her will. I suppose he got the barbiturates from the College.'

'Yes, he'd been a student there himself and knew his way about the place. So having arranged with Kay to fake an alibi, and with Meg away in London, not knowing what he was doing, he went there and got hold of some of the stuff and then went on to join Mrs Cannon just about the time she was making coffee for herself. Probably he gave her a nice surprise by his unexpected visit, and may have stayed chatting to her in the kitchen while she was making the coffee, or may even have sat by her bed for a while, while she was drinking it, and at some point poured the drug into the coffee-pot, then made for home and was waiting there when Meg got back from London.'

'But, Paul, he hadn't time to do that,' Sara said. 'They'd only one car and Meg had taken it away in the morning when she went to catch the train to London. He couldn't possibly have walked from Bolding into Edgewater and across the Heath to the College and then to the Cannons' house and been in time to join Mrs Cannon over her coffee, apart from actually getting home again before Meg.'

'He had the twins' bicycles, hadn't he? They were in London, they weren't going to want them. And on a bicycle I think he could have done it quite easily. He'd have had to stay up at the farm with the men who were working on the harvesting until it seemed reasonable for him to go in for his lunch, but then he could have shot straight off on a bike to the College and then to the Cannons' house. And he'd got his alibi fixed that he'd been at the farm all the afternoon.'

'And that's where we get to my answerphone,' Sara said.

'Yes, the mistake that ruined everything for him. But d'you know what I'd like to know? When Kay agreed to make that telephone call for him, knowing that it was to prove that he was at the farm when in fact he wouldn't be there, did she know that it would be because he was committing a murder? I can't help wondering about that. She seemed really quite a nice sort of girl, not very bright, but somehow not a murderous type. But we'll never know about that. I've a feeling that perhaps she didn't really understand what she'd done until Mrs Cannon died and it was only as she began to take in what had happened that she got that migraine we've all heard about. A very convenient migraine, but perhaps it was a real one, brought on by the discovery that she'd been having an affair with a murderer. Or perhaps she simply had to have a day at home to think about what she ought to do, now that she began to understand the position. And then after the General's death she decided to tell you about it. Again, we'll never be quite sure why, except that you were the only person who knew for sure about the tape on the answerphone and it may have been that she meant to beg you not to say it could have been her voice on the tape, or perhaps she was simply going to say that whatever you said about it, she'd deny it. You'd no witness, after all. But I think it was that call to you that brought about her own death.'

'Because Ron came in when she was making the call and killed her there and then. Her garden door would probably have been open on a hot evening like that, and he could simply have walked in.'

Paul nodded. 'He'd lost his wits by then and didn't know what to do but to go on and on murdering.'

'But why did he murder the General?'

'Didn't the General make a call to the farm in the evening after you and he had been there? And didn't he phone you later to say he thought he understood the answerphone problem? Well, if he'd said that to Ron, and perhaps even asked him to come and see him to discuss it, never dreaming that he himself would be in danger, wouldn't that have been enough to drive Ron over the edge? The strain of having committed one murder may already have been rather more than he had bargained for. For all we know, of course, he may really have been over the edge for much longer than any of us realized. There was something not quite normal about his passion for those children. Perhaps that ought to have warned us.'

'I think I understand the General's call,' Sara said. 'He believed me about the message on the answerphone, so he felt sure, when Ron said he'd received a message just like it at the farm, that he was lying. Of course, Kay might have made a second call to the farm which Ron could have received if he'd been there, but that still wouldn't have explained the message on the tape.'

'And if they hadn't gone in for all that elaboration, no one would have doubted very seriously that Mrs Cannon committed suicide, and the other murders, for which Ron will be sentenced, wouldn't have been necessary,' Paul said. 'But as we've agreed, they arranged beforehand that Kay was to make the call in front of the girl who shared her office and behave as if she was getting an answer, and they must have arranged more or less what she was to say, then Ron could say he'd had the call and be able to repeat what the girl had heard, and that would be his alibi, if one was needed. Of course Kay ought to have warned Ron not to say that he'd ever received the message, but as we've agreed, she wasn't very bright. If he hadn't done that, the General might have been very puzzled about the whole thing, but he wouldn't have had any suspicion of him.'

'Paul, has it struck you that our friend the constable dropped a pretty broad hint that it might have been you who got hold of the drug for Mrs Cannon?' Sara said. 'He said that there are all sorts of ways of getting hold of drugs these days, as you yourself must know. Wasn't he thinking of your brother?'

'Suppose he was,' Paul said, 'does it matter?'

'Not very much, I imagine.'

'Does it matter to you?'

'No.'

'Are you sure?' He gave a long look into her eyes.

She met it with an equally long look and shook her head.

'Quite sure,' she said.

'Then that's all right.'

'But there's no proof of anything,' she said. 'Of anything at all.'

'None at all.'

'And if we're wrong . . .'

'Just find a better explanation for everything that's happened,' Paul said, 'and I'll listen.'

The memoirs of Mary Markle and of Montgomery the mule were written that winter. Sara became very good friends with the aged writer, though at times, when she looked at the worn, wrinkled face with the excellent grey wig above it, usually comfortably supported on a colourful sofa cushion, she would be visited by an appalling conviction that the old woman was certain to die suddenly before the work was finished. Her death, of course, would be entirely natural. There would be no question about that. And the feeling never visited Sara for more than a moment. Actually Mary Markle, who, like so many other people, claimed to have had a very interesting life, but who felt too tired to write about it herself, lived to attend a luncheon at which the book was launched, and to give Sara and Paul a wedding present which consisted of a model of Montgomery in bronze, specially commissioned from a little known sculptor whom Mary Markle was proud to have discovered living in a cottage in the Highlands of Scotland.

Sara and Paul thanked her warmly, then although they admired the mule very much, they gave it away on the quiet as a prize at a fête for an animal charity in which a friend of theirs happened to be involved. There are events in the lives of every one of us of which we do not wish to possess a constant reminder.